T0130575

Into the Sweet Hereafter

Books by Kaye George

Vintage Sweets Mysteries
Revenge is Sweet
Deadly Sweet Tooth
Into the Sweet Hereafter

Published by Kensington Publishing Corporation

Into the Sweet Hereafter

Kaye George

LYRICAL PRESS
Kensington Publishing Corp.
www.kensingtonbooks.com

LYRICAL PRESS BOOKS are published by

Kensington Publishing Corp.
119 West 40th Street
New York, NY 10018

All Kensington titles, imprints, and distributed lines are available at special quantity discounts for bulk purchases for sales promotion, premiums, fund-raising, educational, or institutional use.

Special book excerpts or customized printings can also be created to fit specific needs. For details, write or phone the office of the Kensington Sales Manager: Kensington Publishing Corp., 119 West 40th Street, New York, NY 10018. Attn. Sales Department. Phone: 1-800-221-2647.

Lyrical Press and Lyrical Press logo Reg. U.S. Pat. & TM Off.

First Electronic Edition: March 2021
ISBN-13: 978-1-5161-0542-7 (ebook)
ISBN-10: 1-5161-0542-7 (ebook)

First Print Edition: March 2021
ISBN-13: 978-1-5161-0545-8
ISBN-10: 1-5161-0545-1

Printed in the United States of America

I want to dedicate this book to all of my family and friends who kept in touch during the pandemic, when I was writing this. I think we all helped to save each other's sanity. I loved having this project to take me away from the real world.

Prologue

Outside, the sun pressed toward the horizon. The tourists on Mandalay Hill, unfazed by the 100-degree heat, watched the sun set over the sparkling Irrawaddy River below.

Inside the factory, the heat was even more intense. It didn't seem to bother the two men, but their argument had raised the temperature even higher for everyone else within earshot. They both spoke Burmese, as many in Mandalay did. In English, their conversation would have gone something like this.

"You're trying to do it too cheap, Uncle Win."

"Stop. Stand still." Uncle Win's voice was deep, rumbling.

Thet Thura, who had been pacing the new cement floor of the plant, halted in front of the older man. "This is important. The first business of this kind in Myanmar, Uncle. I don't want it to fail."

"Do you think I want it to fail?" The older man, Min Win, known to many as U Win, looked up at his taller young relative. "It will not fail. Why do you think it would? The plastic has to decompose. It has to fall apart after you use it. That's the whole point. Making it cheaper makes it better. It will break down sooner."

Thet bowed his head, acknowledging the words of his elder. He stood waiting for U Win to depart for the day. When he was gone, Thet summoned his cousins, who had been waiting nearby. The two cousins ran to him, each toting a large burlap bag, and they got to work on their covert mission. U Win knew all about the scheme—he had masterminded everything in the beginning—but he didn't want to appear to be involved.

The last batch of plastic for the day was being produced, but Thet halted the clanking machines so he and his cousins could add an extra step to the process. The burlap bag held one of the most precious substances in Myanmar, the country that used to be called Burma, and still was by many. The men reached into the bag and pulled out handfuls of beautiful, smooth, Burma jadeite, the best jade in the world. One of the cousins had to hold up an emerald-colored, almost translucent stone to admire it before he proceeded. The Chinese called this the Stone of Heaven.

The young men were surrounded by large, drab, gray machines that had been noisy all day and now lay silent, like crouching lizards, ready to spring into action again. The smells of oiled motors, new plastic, and the sweat of the departed workers hung in the air. The jade was the brightest spot in the factory.

The jade mines in Myanmar were controlled by cruel overlords. Locals worked hard to dig out the valuable rock, eking out a meager existence. They were searched when they left every day, to prevent them from smuggling out the jade. Thet was an enterprising young man, though. He had hatched a plan to bribe one of the guards and smuggle the jade to the United States, where it could be sold on the black market to enrich the guard, himself, and Thet's extended family. The first bribe had to be done from his own pocket, but he had completed two cycles now. The third shipment, which should go out tomorrow, would start to show him a profit.

The three men worked quickly, inserting the stones into plastic replicas of American candies, then sealing the seams, making sure they marked the boxes the fake candies were put into.

They were joined by two more cousins. One of them had always been slow. Thet had to oversee his work at first, but he seemed to know what to do now. Thet would prefer not to employ that cousin, but knew he had to work with him. That's what families did.

A few hours later, the entire batch of plastic was finished and loaded onto a truck to be eventually transported to an aquarium shop in Dallas, which served as Thet's front for the backroom smuggling operation. The plan was for the shipment to fly over the Pacific, as usual, a shipment of innocent-looking, new, eco-friendly compostable plastic. It would be trucked from the airplane to a warehouse in west Texas, then brought to Dallas.

It wasn't until the next morning that Thet consulted his notes and realized, with a sickening jolt, his cousin had inserted the jade into the wrong batch of plastic. This batch wasn't bound for his aquarium shop in Dallas, but, after going to the warehouse outside a small Texas town called Fredericksburg, it would be trucked to an address very close by, a place called Bella's Baskets. The shipment without the jade was going to his shop in Dallas. This was very, very wrong. He had to make sure the jade-filled plastic didn't get to Bella's Baskets.

Thet Thura got to Texas as quickly as he could. He flew to San Antonio, then things got a bit more complicated. He usually flew to Dallas and didn't know this part of Texas. He asked a few people how best to get to his destination and decided to get a private plane to the tiny airport outside the small town that served the county. From there, he rented a car and drove to the warehouse that he hoped still held the precious cargo his stupid cousin had mislabeled. He knew his uncle, U Win, would blame Thet for the error, since he was in charge of the smuggling. U Win pretended to everyone that he didn't know what his nephews were doing, though he was behind the scheme. He had Thet carry out the operation so it looked like he was in charge.

When Thet got to the warehouse, he didn't want to make inquiries that people would remember. But he had to find out where his shipment was. He had thought of an approach on his long flight over the Pacific. He needed to call his associate in Dallas as soon as he landed. The associate, Arlen Snead, said he could meet him in the town of Fredericksburg, but Thet would have to intercept the load before Arlen arrived.

Thet parked his rental car at the edge of the large lot and walked toward the prefab metal building. One truck was in the process of backing up to the loading dock. He strolled to the driver's side and waited for the man to alight from the cab.

"Can you help me?" he asked. His accent was slight, from having done business in Dallas for several years and also from having a good ear for languages.

The trucker stopped and said, "Howdy. What do you need?" He had dark skin and black, curly hair. He wore a cotton company shirt with the Planet Earth logo and the name "Mateo" on the pocket.

"I need to hire a truck driver for a single job," Thet said. "A small one. Do you know of anyone who would want to pick up an extra job?"

"Where to? Who's it for?"

"I can't say too much." Thet looked down at his shoes. "It would be unofficial. Off the books. Cash-based." He knew, from working with Arlen, that these code words would tell the man it wasn't quite legal. He didn't want to hire an honest truck driver. He needed one who was hungry and would jump at any job. And keep his mouth shut.

The man tilted his head back and looked hard at Thet Thura, squinting to indicate he knew what they were talking about. "I might know someone," he said. "What would it pay?"

"We can decide that after I tell the person what is involved."

"I'm your person. Let's talk."

1

Tally Holt opened her eyes to the startlingly close orbs of her big Maine coon cat, Nigel. He stared earnestly, communicating his desire for breakfast. How did he do that? she wondered. How did she know what he was thinking? By his sheer willpower, she assumed. He had enough of that. She smiled and rubbed the top of his velvet head, starting his purring motor. She loved the volume he put out.

"Move, silly, so I can get the sheet off me." She shoved him gently so she could peel back the one sheet and sit up. It was too warm to use covers, really, but she always felt better when she was covered with something.

Nigel padded after her into the kitchen of her small Fredericksburg house, chirping, Tally was sure, to indicate the degree of urgency that existed. He needed to eat, he was letting her know, and he needed to eat *now*. Sunlight poured in through the windows, filtered by the old live oaks in the front yard. Later, when the relentless Texas Hill Country sun rose higher, the trees would shade the whole house. After she scooped the cat food into his dish and refilled his water bowl, she cleaned the litter while he crunched his noisy way through the bowl of kibble.

Cats are so easy, she thought. That had taken less than five minutes and he was set until tonight.

She hadn't grown up with any pets, but knew, from observation, that dogs required a lot more maintenance. It had been a long time since the day she got mad at her brother, Cole, for dumping Nigel on her. He had broken up with one of his many girlfriends and the jilted woman hadn't taken Nigel with her.

Tally had to admit, she liked to come home to a warm, living being at night after she closed up her shop. Before that happened today, though, she had to get dressed and actually open up that shop.

Soon she was blowing an ignored kiss to Nigel and heading out the front door.

* * * *

Tally and her best friend Yolanda Bella beamed as they stood on the warm sidewalk outside Bella's Baskets in Fredericksburg, Texas, where the tourist season was moving into high gear. They were delighted with the window display Yolanda had just finished putting together.

Tally turned to her favorite employee. "Lily, the new plastic candies look exactly like the real thing. They're wonderful."

The plastic replicas of the vintage sweets that Tally sold next door at Tally's Olde Tyme Sweets were nestled in an assortment of gift baskets, some handmade locally, some bought and reconditioned by Yolanda herself. Lily Vale, Tally's young employee, had come up with the idea to use replicas in Yolanda's displays last year. The ones they'd been using had become faded, dull, and old-looking from being exposed to the fierce Texas sun coming through the window, so Lily had set out to find another place to buy the replicas. She had searched sources all over the world before finally deciding on this one. The fake candies were made in Southeast Asia from custom molds modeled after sketches Lily had submitted. They were not only much cheaper, but they were environmentally friendly, according to the ads.

"I'm glad they got here so soon," Lily said. "You know, this is kind of a celebration of your one-year mark." Her brown eyes sparkled, showing just how happy she was for her boss.

"It's that long already? A year?" Tally hadn't realized that. It *was* a year ago, mid-June, when she had opened her shop with high hopes, which, for the most part, had panned out. Her shop and Yolanda's were both thriving, after some early struggles. She swelled with pride, looking over the colorful display that married her vintage candy products and Yolanda's beautiful gift baskets.

The colorful baskets held items to go with the themes people usually wanted: birthday (candles, party hats, small gifts wrapped in birthday paper), anniversary (photo albums, silk roses, tin stars in a ten-year basket and silver stars in a twenty-five-year one), and the celebration of moving into a new house (small houses from a toy store, bags of grass seed for the new lawns, Monopoly dollar bills).

Strewn among the baskets were boughs from dogwood trees bursting with white silk blossoms, and a few pink silk crape myrtles, since it was spring in Texas Hill Country.

Chattering people strolled past, perusing the displays of the touristy shops of Fredericksburg and enjoying a soft, warm day before summer descended upon the town in earnest. Of course, that meant it was in the high eighties, not yet the nineties—temperatures that would not be merely considered "warm" in other parts of the country. Even the full summer heat would not deter the tourists and local shoppers, however. The small German-founded town was a popular shopping, dining, and wine-tasting destination for much of the year.

Tally's landlady, Mrs. Gerg, in her worn, ill-fitting shoes, shuffled up to the group—Tally, Yolanda, and the other two—Raul Fuentes, Yolanda's trusted assistant in the basket shop, and Lily Vale, Tally's dependable employee in the vintage sweet shop.

"My, doesn't that look nice." Mrs. Gerg stuck her head forward to peer at the display. Tally could see her pink scalp through the short, curly hairdo the older woman wore. Tally was only a few inches over five feet, but Mrs. Gerg was even shorter.

"Aren't you afraid the chocolate will melt on those Whoopie Pies?" Mrs. Gerg asked. "They look so much more like the real thing, better than those plastic ones you were using." She gave Tally a worried look. "It's warm, and the sun is hitting the window full-on right now." She was right about that. The afternoon sun's rays were shining directly onto the baskets, the better for everyone to see them.

Tally smiled and waved a hand toward Lily. "Don't worry—they aren't real—they're biodegradable plastic replicas. We can thank Lily for them. This was all her idea and she found a very reasonable place to get them."

"Compostable, really," Lily added.

Mrs. Gerg took another look at the goodies, which were glistening through the glass. "So they are. Very good, Lily. How clever of you. They look like the real thing."

Lily beamed. Tally noticed the way Raul was looking at the young woman. His brown eyes were big and adoring. Lovestruck. Was this new? Tally had never noticed the attraction between the two of them before. Lily returned a similar moonstruck gaze to the dark, handsome young man. It might be new, but it was mutual. Tally decided they looked good together. Lily, with her lithe dancer's build, was half a head taller than the slim, compact Raul, which didn't seem to bother either one of them a bit.

Some of the passersby also paused to admire the wares, creating a bit of a blockage in the flow of foot traffic. One man, hobbling past on a pair of crutches, stopped, too, staring at the window intently. He looked unhappy—or maybe angry—about something, his brow furrowed, his lips pursed.

Tally followed his gaze and took a harder look at the replicas. Some of them looked lopsided. Were they melting? The spring sun that shone on Fredericksburg could be as hot as a full summer sun in a lot of other places.

Yes, something was wrong. But the pieces were only slightly misshapen. Should they take them out of the window before they got worse? Maybe they would last through the week, and then Tally and Yolanda would decide what to do. Put them somewhere else? Get a refund for faulty replicas?

The man on crutches noticed Tally paying attention to him and quickly turned to stump a few steps away on one good foot and his crutches.

Yolanda sneezed three times in a row, whipping a tissue out of her pocket. Tally knew she kept them ever-present in the spring for her pollen allergies.

"How's the crime watch going for y'all, Mrs. Gerg?" Yolanda asked, tucking her tissue back into her pocket. Mrs. Gerg was a member of the newly founded neighborhood group calling themselves Crime Fritzers, after a popular nickname for Fredericksburg, Fritztown.

"It's getting off the ground." Mrs. Gerg grinned at the younger women. "We're determined to keep crime down in our beautiful city."

Tally didn't think the crime rate was very high at the moment, but fighting it gave Mrs. Gerg something constructive to do and kept her from a hobby of hers, which was, unfortunately, collecting piles of things from garage and yard sales around town to give to Tally. Tally was running out of room to store the cheap treasures Mrs. Gerg delighted in bringing her. She hadn't received any in three weeks, since the Crime Fritzers started their organized patrols, so Tally was in favor of the group.

Mrs. Gerg walked away in her ancient shoes with run-down heels. She had walked miles in them during the time Tally knew her, so Tally had quit worrying about her feet, as she had when she first knew the woman.

Lily lurched forward, shoved from behind by a careless pedestrian. The offender hurried off without saying "excuse me" and Tally caught Lily so she wouldn't fall into the plate glass window.

"Are you all right?"

Lily straightened up. "I'm fine." She winced.

"Is your back hurt?" Tally held her arm lightly, to make sure she stayed upright.

"I think I took an elbow, but it'll be okay."

"You're sure? I can get you some ice."

Lily waved Tally off. "No, no, I'm fine. Really. But I'm going to call Planet Earth about this." She pointed to the piece of plastic that was melting the fastest. It glistened and looked sticky. "They need to give us a refund."

"I think that guy hit you with his crutch," said Raul, gently touching Lily's back, where she'd been pushed. Lily turned to face Raul and gave him a radiant smile.

Tally saw the concern on Raul's face as the two lovebirds gazed at each other. Yes, there was something there, and that something was sizzling across the air between them.

* * * *

Yolanda and Raul soon went back inside Bella's Baskets and Tally and Lily returned to Tally's Olde Tyme Sweets to continue their workday.

Tally wondered if she would ever tire of walking into her shop through the front door. Everything she had done with it had worked, in her opinion. The soft chime to indicate the door was open, ideally to tell them that a customer had entered. The walls, done in muted, swirling pinks and lilacs on the walls, the gleaming glass cases full of sweet treats and candies for the day. She loved even the things she hadn't changed—the wide-plank wooden flooring and the cute overhead lights with Mason jars for shades.

Molly Kelly was holding down the fort; that is, the salesroom in the front of the sweet shop, waiting on a group of Red Hat ladies who wanted treats for their next meeting. The local Red Hat Society had a large chapter and Tally was glad when they'd decided to use her shop as their official treat supplier for their meetings a few months back.

Tally paused a moment to take in the blended scents of her candies, chocolate, caramel, baked goods, even a whiff of peanut butter, before she retired to the kitchen, which was behind the salesroom, to whip up a batch of Mallomars. She had noticed that the glass display case was low on them. In the front, she saw Lily tie on her pink smock, designed to match the wall colors, and greet the next group to come through the front door and sound the chime, three teenage boys who looked hungry. It was too noisy to hear the ticking of the clock on the wall, fashioned to look like a little fat baker wearing an apron, his hands pointing to the minutes and hours.

A little later, Tally was dipping caramel squares in warm chocolate and setting them on waxed paper when Molly shuffled into the kitchen with her shoulders slumped, her head down. Tally tried to read her expression. "Are you okay, Molly?" It didn't seem like it.

Molly hung her head even lower and, since she was shorter than Tally's five-three, obscured her face. Tally pulled a stool out at the granite-topped island where she stood working. "Take a load off, Molly. Tell me what's bothering you. If I can't help, I can listen."

Molly raised her head and gave her a hopeful look. "That sounds nice." She climbed up onto the stool and rested an elbow on the countertop, letting her cheek drop onto her fist. "I don't really know. I think things are just piling up."

"How is your mom's treatment going?" Tally knew her mother was being treated for cancer, but she thought the woman was expected to recover.

Molly shrugged. "Okay, I guess. But it's hard on her."

"Are you worried about your dad?"

"I always worry about him."

Her father, an auto mechanic, had hurt his back at work and was on disability. Tally wasn't sure of his status. "Is he on disability forever now? Or can he go back to work some day?"

"He can't work on cars," Molly said, lifting her head off her fist, finally. "He and Mom fight. She thinks he should do something else. He doesn't think he can. And Howie, well…"

"What does Howie say?" Howie, a mechanic who worked where Molly's father used to, might know more. Molly was dating Howie, as far as Tally knew.

Molly shrugged again. "We don't talk about him lately." She screwed her face up and squeezed a couple of tears out of each very blue eye. "We… don't talk…about…anything."

"Are you not seeing each other?" Tally hoped that wasn't true. They were an ideal couple and had seemed very much in love.

Molly gave one last shrug, wiped her eyes with her apron, and jumped off the stool to return to the front of the store. That was too bad. It seemed they were on the outs.

Tally wasn't sure that session had done poor Molly any good. She finished the caramels and went into the office to work on paperwork there.

* * * *

"Can I use the phone in here?" Lily asked, poking her head into the office door during a lull in customer traffic. "I want to call that place."

"What place?" Tally wondered why she wouldn't use her cell phone.

"Plastic Earth."

"You mean Planet Earth?"

"Oh yeah, Planet Earth Plastics. It sounds funny saying I'm calling Planet Earth, doesn't it?"

They both giggled. Tally stuck around to listen to the call, curious about what Lily would say and how she would conduct herself. It turned out that she didn't say anything or conduct herself at all because the company didn't answer her call.

"I guess there's a time difference, right?" Lily said, giving up reluctantly.

"It's on the other side of the world, so probably."

"Maybe I'll just email or write."

They both perked up at the chime of the front door opening, telling them that some customers had just entered.

"I'll do it tomorrow," Lily said, and headed for the salesroom.

At a few minutes past seven, after cleaning up the shop, Tally closed up and walked the few blocks through the warm evening to the house she rented from Mrs. Gerg, on East Schubert Street. The crape myrtles, planted in depressions in the sidewalks, weren't blooming yet, but their branches were full of lush green leaves, rustling in a slight breeze Tally was grateful for. It lifted her straight hair off her damp neck.

Nigel, that huge black-and-white tuxedo Maine coon cat, greeted her at the door. If he were a dog, his tail would be wagging. As it was, he started talking to her in his cheerful chirps, no doubt inquiring about din-din time.

"Soon," Tally reassured him. "I just need to get my slippers on and pour a glass of iced tea. Then I'll get you something to eat."

Now, in the early part of June, the temperature was still in the high sixties this time of night. She'd gotten warm walking home. After they had both eaten, she took him into the backyard in his harness.

"Look, Nige." She gazed skyward and pointed above, through the small, tough leaves of the live oak. "There's a full moon tonight. Isn't it beautiful?"

For just a moment, she felt sorry for herself, being outside under a romantic full moon, the smell of jasmine on the fence next door wafting into her yard on the slight breeze, with a cat as her only companion. But the thought of Raul and Lily and the glowing looks they'd given each other brought a smile to her lips. Molly and Howie were another matter, but they had dated for a long time now. Tally thought they would probably get back

together. The perfect evening seemed to call for thoughts of romance, even
if it wasn't her romance.

* * * *

Yolanda Bella arrived at Bella's Baskets on Friday in a good mood. In
the last few years, she'd had many differences with her overbearing father,
who didn't think she had what it took to make her business succeed. But
last night she'd taken a check over to the ranch her parents owned on the
outskirts of town.

When he opened the front door, she stuck the check out. "This will
repay one fourth of what I've borrowed from you," she said.

She got a kick out of his blank stare. He took the check and looked at
the amount, then frowned. "Can you afford this?"

She twisted a strand of her glossy dark hair, trying to act nonchalant.
This was a big moment for her, but she didn't want him to know that. "I
said I'd repay you, and I am."

"I don't want you to run out of cash," he said.

That was exactly her problem, right there. He always thought she
needed rescuing, needed to be taken care of. What she *needed* was to be
treated as an adult.

"I'll let you know when I have the next payment." She had driven
away, pleased with herself. She hadn't taken any of his bait, had remained
calm. And the truth was, she *could* afford the amount she had given him.
Business was very good.

The next morning, if she'd known how to whistle, she would have been
whistling as she came through the back door, greeted by the heady smell
of lilies. The whiff she took tickled her nose and brought out a couple of
big sneezes.

Her employee must have laid the bunch of lilies on the counter earlier.
He was now at the front of the shop.

"Miss Yolanda!" Raul summoned her, sounding frantic, and she ran to
the front. He looked stricken. "Look what happened."

Bright sunlight streamed through her display window. Then she noticed
the rays glinting off a few small shards of shattered glass on the sidewalk
outside. The window was broken.

* * * *

Heading down the sidewalk to open her store, Tally Holt saw a commotion ahead.

"Tally, look!" Yolanda, standing outside the front of her store, shouted and waved her forward. She sounded distraught.

When Tally approached, she could see why. The sidewalk before Bella's Baskets sparkled with broken glass. The window had been smashed.

"What happened?" Tally asked. There hadn't been a storm. Someone must have broken it, but why? She heard a crunch and realized she had stepped on some glass fragments with her sneakers.

"Somebody threw a rock through my window," Yolanda wailed.

Tally took a good look, as well as she could, through the police personnel photographing and measuring. There was a lot more glass inside, looking like ice crystals on the contents of the baskets.

"They're gone!" Yolanda pointed at the window.

"What's gone?" Tally looked more closely, then she saw it. The new plastic replicas were gone. There were no puddles where they had been, though. They hadn't melted. They were missing completely.

Who would steal cheap plastic pieces of candy? Pieces that were falling apart?

And why did the window smell so lovely? Tally peered inside the store and saw Raul, who had gone back to arranging some stargazer lilies on the work counter. That's what she smelled, the lilies.

Detective Jackson Rogers emerged from the knot of police personnel. "Tally, you and Yolanda come over here. I need to let you know what happened."

They joined him a few feet away from the growing crowd. "It looks like someone stole the plastic candies," Tally said. "Is that right?"

"Yes, to begin with." Detective Rogers glanced at the notepad he was holding. "At four in the morning, a member of the local crime watchers group observed a brick being thrown through the window and one party scooping up the plastic pieces."

"Oh, so you caught the thief?"

"Tally, stop interrupting me." Jackson's words were stern, but he smiled when he said them. His gray eyes, that could be hard as steel, matched his warm smile at the moment. He grew more serious as he continued, though. "The crime watcher was beaten and the thief escaped with the goods. We got a description and think we should be able to apprehend him soon."

"Someone got beat up?" Yolanda put a hand to her mouth. "Was it bad?"

"He's in the hospital." The detective looked at his notes. "A member of the neighborhood watch group."

"A 'he' and not a 'she'? For sure?" Tally asked. "Not Mrs. Gerg? She's a member of that group. They go walking on patrol through the downtown at night."

Jackson gave his head a slight shake. "We've asked them to stay in their vehicles. They're also not supposed to apprehend anyone. Unfortunately, this is what can happen when they disregard our recommendations. But no, it was not Mrs. Gerg. It's a member of her group, though. It's the..." he consulted his notes again "...Crime Fritzers. Another thing we've told them is that they're not supposed to be alone. They are always supposed to patrol in pairs."

"Yes, that's her group. And the injured man was in the group? In the Crime Fritzers?"

The detective smiled. "Crime Fritzers. Yeah." He chuckled, a brief twinkle hitting his gray eyes. "Sorry. Funny name."

Tally had to smile, too.

"But y'all don't have the thieves," Yolanda said. "Does anyone have any idea why they were stealing those pieces of plastic? They're not expensive."

"They're a little too cheap, in fact," Tally said. "Lily ordered them because they were economical and environmentally friendly. But it turns out that means they dissolve. And way too quickly."

"Really?" Yolanda turned to her. "Y'all didn't tell me that."

"Did you notice they were starting to melt yesterday in the sun?" Tally said. "I asked Lily about them last night before we closed. She had noticed they were melting, too, but didn't want to say anything. She hoped they would hold up. I thought they would, too. I was going to leave them a few more days. In fact, she tried to call the company, but couldn't get them to answer the phone."

Yolanda threw her head back. Tally thought she might be asking for strength from above.

"I know, Yo. We should have just taken them out."

"Are you finished?" Jackson asked. "I need to get back to work." He walked over to a large, burly officer Tally recognized as Officer Edwards. It looked like he was leading the physical, forensic investigation. From her experience with him, she knew she could trust Edwards to be thorough and fair, no matter what turned up, since he had always been so in the past.

"Wait," Tally said. "Is there any reason he wanted to steal them?"

"We're working on that," the detective said, and walked off, leaving Tally and Yolanda looking at each other, perplexed.

"I wonder when we can clean up this mess," Yolanda said.

Tally saw one of the crime scene people swabbing a piece of the broken glass. It had a dark substance on it. Blood? Had the person who broke the window gotten cut? Maybe they could get DNA from that. If they would bother with DNA tests for such a cheap theft.

When Tally told her workers what had happened, Molly said, "I can get hold of Ozzy. He can do the glass really fast. I'll call him right now."

Tally had no idea who Ozzy was, but thanked Molly. "I'll call Yolanda and tell her."

The crime scene tape came down at about noon and Yolanda called Tally, whose shop had opened nearly on time and was doing a booming business. Probably, Tally thought, because the crime team with their bright yellow tape was a draw for curiosity seekers. Once they had checked out the basket shop activity, they naturally walked next door and were lured into the sweet shop.

"Can y'all spare a minute, or one of your workers, to help me get my window space cleaned up?" Yolanda asked Tally when she answered her cell phone. "I have someone coming later today to put in a new piece of glass."

"Ozzy, right? You got same-day service. Great. I can come myself. I think everyone in town has been here today already, so it's slowing down now."

Three young women currently worked for Tally. Molly Kelly and Lily Vale worked every day but Monday, the day the shop was closed. Her third employee, Dorella Diggs, came in Wednesdays and Fridays. On those days, Tally could afford to take time away from the shop.

Tally called to her employees that she was going out to help Yolanda. "I might as well do some shopping for the store, if there's time after that."

"Will you be back by closing?" Lily asked from behind the counter, where she was ringing up a sale on a bag of Mallomars.

"I'm not sure. It's a mess, with all the broken glass. Can you just close up if I'm not back by seven?"

"Sure. Don't worry about it. My cousin is working late, too." Lily had been living with her parents, but they had moved away and she was living in an apartment with her cousin Amy, who worked in the office at a real estate company.

Tally assured her that she wouldn't worry about it. She had, finally, three dependable, trustworthy women working for her. It made her life easy.

As she walked up to the window where Yolanda was leaning into the opening, carefully picking glass shards off the floor of the display space, a white pickup pulled up and parked nose-in at the curb. A magnetic sign on the side of it advertised *Ozzy's Odd Jobs* with a local phone number in bright red lettering.

A small man jumped out. He was compact and wiry, probably in his forties, and had a horseshoe mustache, coming down to his chin on either side of his mouth. "Which one is Mizz Bella?" He looked at Tally first and she pointed to Yolanda.

Yolanda straightened up and dusted her hands off on her bright yellow skirt. She had topped it, in her characteristic fashion, with an orange, scoop-necked peasant blouse. "You brought the window already? Great."

Tally stared at him. Molly was right. Ozzy was very, very fast. She would have to ask her how she knew him. He was a handy guy to know.

He unclipped a large piece of clear glass from the holder on the side of his truck.

Tally whispered to Yolanda, having doubts in spite of being impressed by his speed. "Are you sure it's the right size? How did he know how big a piece of glass to bring?"

Yolanda laughed. "He came and measured right away. Right after Molly called him."

Tally nodded, reassured. "Yes, that's good then. I'm glad she mentioned him."

"Wait just a sec," Yolanda said. "We need to get the rest of this debris out of here." She dashed inside and came back with a large paper bag, a small whisk broom, and a dustpan. She and Tally scooped up what was left of the broken glass, taking care not to cut their fingers. Then Yolanda swept the bottom and poured the debris into the large bag. Tally spotted some other detritus, some dull pieces of things that weren't broken glass. She leaned farther into the window and decided they were pieces of a broken plastic Whoopie Pie. As she picked them up, shiny green stones fell out. She gathered those, too, and stuck everything into Yolanda's bag. Maybe the stones were inside the plastic pieces to weigh them down or something. But it was curious that they were so pretty. She wanted to look at them more closely later, when she had time. They would be able to finish removing the baskets and other decor from inside later, but this cleanup of the bottom was much easier from the front.

"Okay, we're done." Yolanda gestured toward the open space with the shards of remaining broken window glass clinging to the edges.

Ozzy moved with precision and speed and had the broken pieces removed from the window frame and the window glass replaced in what seemed like minutes, as Tally and Yolanda watched. After he finished, he said he'd send a bill.

The two women stood looking for a moment at what was left of the display. The baskets remained, full of goodies and beribboned to match their themes. The dogwood and crape myrtle boughs were still there, too, and undamaged.

"I guess I have to redo the whole window now," Yolanda said.

"I don't think you need to do that. It doesn't look that bad. You should pick the tiny pieces of glass out of them, I think. But they look okay. It's just that the candies are missing. If you didn't know they'd been there, you wouldn't think anything is wrong. We have a few more we didn't use, don't we?"

"Not enough."

"You're right. They would look lonely if we put them in there."

"That's it, lonely," Yolanda said. "I'm exhausted. You want to get a snack?"

"Yes, I can do that. I didn't know how long this would take so I told the girls I might not be back. But your shop is still open. Can you leave?"

"Ha. You notice I haven't had any customers since you came. It's nearly closing time anyway. I'll run inside, stash this bag, and tell Raul to close up. Let's go celebrate surviving the Broken Window Incident."

Tally grinned. "Let's do that."

2

After Tally checked on the employees closing up her shop, she waited outside while Yolanda went inside Bella's Baskets for her purse. An older sedan, so dark blue it was almost black, pulled up. Two men got out and approached Tally, appearing friendly. It was just before seven, so the sky was still bright. The sun wouldn't set for another hour and a half. Tally felt the heat radiating up from the sidewalk as the men walked over to her. One of the men was older, heavyset and balding, with a belly that, from the front, made it impossible to tell whether or not he wore a belt. The younger one was taller, but fit looking and had a full head of hair. She recognized the younger man as the son of the new fire chief, since he had picked Dorella up from work twice. Tally assumed he and her employee were dating, now that Dorella and Tally's brother Cole were no longer seeing each other. When Armand Mann was hired as the fire chief from the Dallas Fire Department, the local paper had done an interview with pictures of the family. The size of the fire chief's son and his longish blond hair reminded Tally of Thor from the first time she saw him. But without the hammer. Their car idled, nose in at the curb, as the regular traffic passed by.

The fire chief's son was the first to speak, introducing himself to both women. "Hi, I'm Ira Mann. My partner and I want to reassure you that the Crime Fritzers are on top of this." He hadn't actually met Tally, but she had seen him through the window when he picked Dorella up.

"On top of...the broken window? The plastic?" Tally looked at the car again. "You don't have the Crime Fritzers sign on your car."

"No, we're not on official patrol," the other man said in a gravelly smoker's voice.

"Yeah," Ira added. "Unofficial, extra patrol. We've put on extra units for the crime wave."

"Crime wave? What crime wave?" Tally asked.

Yolanda came out in time to hear Ira's statement. "Yeah, what are you talking about? Have other shops had broken windows?"

"Not windows, per se," Ira said. "But a lot of theft is going down. Home robberies, too. We've beefed up patrols to try to catch the perps."

"Okay." Tally said. "Good luck."

"Can we get some intel?" Ira asked.

"We're on our way out," Yolanda said, brushing him off. "The police have all the information."

Yolanda started to hustle Tally away from them, but Tally turned back. She knew Yolanda was aware of Detective Jackson Rogers's dismissive view of the Crime Watch group, but what could it hurt if more people looked into the problem?

"I think that's great," she said to them. "The more help the better."

Yolanda, Tally could tell, was not in favor.

Ira whipped out a notepad. "Okay, then. What can you tell me about this incident?"

Yolanda and Tally looked at each other. Tally pointed and spoke. "Well, this window was broken and some plastic candies were stolen. It doesn't make much sense."

"Time of the incident?" Ira's pencil scribbled across the notebook.

"During the night," Yolanda said.

"You're with the Crime Fritzers?" Tally asked. "Shouldn't you know about this already? One of your members got hurt trying to stop the thief."

"Oh," said the older man, realization dawning on his chubby face. "This is where Walter got beat up."

Ira wrote a few more words. "Thanks for your time." He wrote his phone number on a blank page, ripped it out, and handed it to Tally. "Let us know if anything else comes up."

They had left the car running and the AC-cooled air tumbled out when they opened the doors to climb back in.

After they drove away, Yolanda said, "Anything else? Like what? What's going to come up? What help are they going to be anyway?"

"You never know, but…I think I have to agree with you. Ira doesn't inspire much confidence, does he?"

Raul came out the front door and locked it after himself. "See you tomorrow, Yolanda. Who were you talking to just now? Those guys that drove off?"

"They were part of the crime watch group," Yolanda said. "They thought they could help out, somehow. You know, that Fritzer group."

"I think my cousin is in that. Mateo. He talks about it all the time. Miss Tally, is Lily at work today?"

"Yes, she's going to help close up. You're welcome to go over."

Raul headed for the sweet shop and Yolanda and Tally headed for Otto's to snag an outdoor table.

* * * *

Pleasantly full of Otto's wurst plate, which had been accompanied by a salad of locally grown ingredients (roasted beets, feta, candied pecans, pickled red onion with caraway vinaigrette), and having parted with Yolanda, Tally nestled in the corner of her secondhand navy-blue couch with Nigel. The television news proceeded without her attention as she answered her phone. It was her mother, Nancy Holt.

"Where are you, Mom?" That was usually her first question.

"We're on Gibraltar." Her mother sounded excited, but she always did, wherever in the world it was she and her husband Bob were performing. "They loved our first performance. The open air theater in the Gibraltar Gardens is one of the prettiest venues we've ever had." Her mother was given to expressing herself in superlatives, which Tally found charming. Usually.

"You just got there yesterday. You did a show already?"

"Went straight from the plane to the theater. Our flight was delayed coming in, so we had to rush. But we made it just fine."

Tally's parents, who were musicians, actors, and dancers, did it all, touring most of the year with brief stops back home in Fredericksburg every once in a while.

"Oh no, I'm sorry," Tally said, thinking the rushing around must have been hard.

"It was nothing. We've had delayed flights before. How's Cole?"

Tally hadn't spoken to her brother for over a week, so had no idea.

"Is he still in Tucson?" her mother asked.

"I don't know. He said this one was going to take a while." He had been in Tucson installing one of his sculpture creations when he called.

"Maybe I'll try to call him then. But you're doing okay? The shop is still okay?"

Tally assured her it was. There was no sense worrying her mother about the theft. There was nothing she could do from Europe. "Take it easy, Mom. Give Dad a hug from me."

They made kissy noises over the phone and Tally was soon in bed, trying to sleep and hoping her own windows would be intact in the morning. Ira had said there were home robberies going on. She had always felt perfectly safe here, in her own home. Tonight, she wasn't sure she did.

3

The next morning, as she arrived at work, Tally gave a grateful glance at her unbroken front windows and went inside. As she was sticking her purse into her desk drawer, Lily came into the office from the kitchen.

"Would you look at this email before I send it?" Lily held out a sheet of paper with a letter printed on it. "Do you think it reads okay?" She screwed her mouth to one side self-deprecatingly, but the effect just made her young face, framed by her long red hair, even more charming.

Tally took it and glanced over the computer-printed text. "You're filing a complaint?"

"Well, I don't know if *filing* is the right word. *Registering*? I want the company to know that their product is substandard. It shouldn't melt in the sun like that. I can't call them, so email should work."

Tally started to agree, then thought she remembered seeing the web page Lily had ordered from. "Wait. What did their ad say? Can you pull up their website?" Tally sat and poised her hands over her computer keyboard.

"Yes. Here, I'll show you." Lily leaned in, typed, and brought up the page she had ordered from. She read the screen, then straightened. "Oh," she said, sudden surprise in her words.

"*Compostable*, it says," Tally read. "*Made of newest-generation compostable plastic. The most evolved in the business. Lowest temperatures and shortest times needed for decomposition. None better than ours.*"

"I don't remember reading that," Lily said. "I noticed that they had a local address and I used them because I think buying local is always good."

"It is," Tally said.

"But look at this." She went to the corner of the office and picked up an empty box. "They came in this and it says *Made in Myanmar*, along with all these characters I can't read. That's not exactly local."

"Don't be discouraged. We'll order something else."

"Yeah, something that doesn't return to the earth in days." Lily looked deflated and discouraged.

"They didn't cost that much," Tally said, trying to cheer her up. "Don't worry about it at all. No problem. Okay?" She couldn't step on the initiative Lily showed with her projects. Look how well the web page she designed for the store had turned out, she told herself.

Lily didn't look convinced, but left the office and got to work mixing up a batch of fudge.

In a very few minutes, Tally heard Lily humming in the kitchen. She poked her head out the office door to see a dreamy smile on Lily's face, as she stirred the fudge. She perched on a stool at the island, the bowl clanking a bit on the taupe granite top.

"Did you and Raul go out last night?" she asked.

Lily gaped. "How did you know?"

"Just a hunch." Tally winked before ducking back to tidy her desk. Tally was about to leave the office and get to work so they could open at ten, when Detective Jackson Rogers called on her cell.

"Are you and Yolanda doing okay?"

That's sweet, she thought. *He's checking up on me.*

"Molly called someone she knew and Yolanda already has her new window installed," Tally said.

"I'm glad. So her business won't be interrupted today, too, then."

"The only loss is the plastic candies." She closed the screen she and Lily had been looking at and locked her computer so she could get to work in the kitchen when she finished the call. She reached for her apron smock and tied it on over her cotton shirt and blue jeans, juggling her cell phone.

"I have to tell you, that's pretty strange. They aren't worth stealing, are they?"

"I wouldn't think so. They didn't cost much. In fact, Lily and I were just talking about how they were probably too cheap. She feels bad because they were biodegrading by the second day."

"We will definitely be looking into them more closely. There must be something we're missing."

"Oh, I have one the thief didn't get." She had stuffed it into the paper bag when she and Yolanda cleaned out the window debris. "A broken Whoopie Pie. Do you want to look at it?"

"Are you free for dinner tonight?" She heard the smile in his voice. She was sure he could hear the same sort of smile in hers. "Sure am. What time?"

* * * *

Tally and Detective Jackson Rogers met at the Auslander, one of the most German restaurants in the very German tourist town. Jackson was wearing his usual off duty jeans and T-shirt. He and Tally nearly had matching wardrobes, except for the sizes. His clothing would drown Tally's short frame. But they both preferred casual clothes whenever possible.

"Do you want to see the Whoopie Pie?" Tally started to pull the bag out of her purse. "The remains of it?" She had put it into a smaller bag when she got it from Yolanda to show to Jackson tonight.

"Let's eat first," Jackson said. "I might want to spend some time looking at it."

Tally didn't know that there was that much to see, but left the paper bag in her purse for now. After she had done justice to a plate of *schweineschnitzel* (pork loin) and Jackson had put away a Reuben, he ordered a second beer for himself and asked to see Tally's evidence.

She fished out the paper bag and handed it to him. "Be careful. There might be some pieces of broken glass in there with it."

He looked inside, and after tilting the bag to catch the light, reached inside and pulled out a piece that was about a third of a plastic Whoopie Pie.

"It's sticky," he said. He handled it with his napkin.

"Yes, it was degrading in the sun. Melting."

"It might have captured some fingerprints."

"I guess my mine will be on it."

"Maybe there are some others, too." He set it down and reached into the bag again with a fresh paper napkin from the holder in the middle of the table. "What's this? It's not plastic."

"Oh, I forgot. There were some green stones near the Whoopie Pie. I was going to look at them at home, but didn't get around to it. I stuck them in there so I wouldn't lose them."

Jackson picked up the stone between the tips of his thumb and forefinger with the napkin and held it, turning it and examining it closely. "I think this is jade." It gleamed in the overhead twinkle lights suspended from the ceiling. He tilted his head, peering inside the bag, and the lights glinted off his soft gray eyes, too.

"Jade? What's that doing there? We didn't have any jade in the window."

He picked out another piece of the melting plastic with yet another paper napkin. Another small green stone was stuck to it. "I think the candy must have had the jade inside it."

"Inside?" That was strange, Tally thought. "Why? To weigh it down?"

He shook out some more stones. He squinted, looking at several of the pieces of jade and poking them with the tip of his unused spoon. "This looks like good quality jade. It might be worth quite a bit."

"You're a rock expert?"

"Not rocks, jewelry. And not an expert, but my uncle is. He owned a jewelry shop in Fort Worth for over thirty years. This is gem-quality jade."

"So they aren't merely green rocks, they are...gems? Valuable gems?"

Jackson kept turning the jade pieces over and over. "This is really good stuff. Look at that color. I think it's jadeite. Burma jade, people call it. It's quite distinctive."

The server came to clear their plates. "Do you want dessert?" she asked.

"Do you have any *butterkuchen* left?" Jackson asked.

She did, and she left to get coffee and a slice of the rich, buttermilk pie for them to share.

"Can I pick one up?" Tally pointed to the stones.

"You already have, so go ahead."

Tally picked up one of them. "It's a pretty color, dark green."

"And translucent," Jackson said. "That's a good quality, I've been told. I'll phone my uncle tonight. I'll have to take this. If these are being smuggled, we'll have to look into it." He took a few more napkins and wrapped the stones.

"Smuggled? In the Whoopie Pie?"

Jackson gave a chuckle. "Looks like it. Whoopie Pie jade."

"You called it Burma jade. Lily ordered these from what she thought was a local business, but they came in a box that said Myanmar on it. That's Burma, right? So, you think that's why Yolanda's window was broken? To steal these and get the jade?"

"Makes a lot more sense than stealing plastic Whoopie Pies, Mary Janes, and Mallomars, doesn't it? This is a crazy way to smuggle jade into the US, though, through you and Yolanda."

Tally had to admit he was right.

He grinned at her. "Is there something I don't know about you two? Do you have a nefarious other side?"

She laughed, knowing he was kidding. But this was getting bizarre.

The server put a plate of *butterkuchen*—buttermilk pie—next to the ruined plastic Whoopie Pie, along with two steaming cups of fragrant coffee, and Tally and Jackson picked up their forks, leaving behind thoughts, for the moment, of smuggling and nefarious dark sides.

* * * *

Jackson walked Tally home, the clamor of Main Street receding after they turned toward her house. Her tummy was even more satisfied than it had been after her dinner with Yolanda. Eating with someone special made food taste so much better. She liked going out with Yolanda, but eating with Detective Jackson Rogers made even the water taste good.

"Anything interesting happening at work for you today?" she asked him. His police job continually fascinated her. It was something different almost every day. "Besides our window?"

"Your broken window is the most interesting thing that is going on right now, but there was a wreck just outside town the night before that. It was kind of weird."

"How so?" She enjoyed the sound of his voice, no matter what he was saying. She always wanted him to go on talking. He was often so reticent.

Some of the rays of light from the streetlights made their way through the trees to highlight his face and shoulders briefly here and there.

"A big truck, a semi, ran into a pickup. The troopers were pretty sure the semi driver fell asleep at the wheel."

That didn't sound unusual. Not good, but not uncommon. Or weird. "Was anyone hurt?"

"The pickup driver was. He went to the hospital. Looked like his leg was broken, smashed. But here's what struck me. The pickup driver was yelling at the semi driver when I got there."

"I might have done that, too."

"But you would have called him a bad driver, or...maybe some other things, too, wouldn't you?"

"I sure would." Tally didn't often use colorful language, but she kept it ready in case she needed it. They had reached her house and walked up her sidewalk slowly.

"Yeah, and he was mad. But he kept saying, 'What did you do that for?' Like maybe he'd done it on purpose. And then, just before they took him away in the ambulance, he yelled, 'Now everything's messed up.'"

"Messed up? I guess so."

"It sounded so specific. Like maybe they had plans together? I'm not explaining it well. It just didn't sound like what a normal person would be upset by. He never said anything about him paying for the hospital or his truck, like you or I would."

"Oh yeah. I'd definitely get the insurance info first thing."

"We got that, of course, for our report. Well, the state trooper got it. But the two men didn't mention it."

"Why were you called? You don't do highways."

"The troopers wanted backup because the pickup driver was so belligerent."

They both stepped onto the dark porch that ran across the front of the house. Tally heard a thump from inside. Jackson tensed.

"What was that?"

Tally laughed. "That was Nigel, probably jumping off the couch because he heard us coming."

"I keep forgetting how big that cat is." Jackson put his warm, strong hands on her shoulders.

Tally smiled, knowing what was coming next. And it did. The longest, sweetest kiss she'd had in ages. She felt her toes curl inside her shoes.

As they broke apart, a car cruised slowly past them. It gave Tally a moment of alarm when the passenger peered out the window at them, then the streetlamp lit the magnetic sign on the door: *Crime Fritzers.*

Jackson felt her stiffen and looked around. "Ah, the intrepid neighborhood crime fighters," he said sarcastically. "Now we're all safe."

"Oh come on, they're just trying to help out." She gave them a wave as they continued their patrol.

"I know, I shouldn't complain. The patrols are fine, from the cars. We're not in favor of them doing it on foot, though. That can lead to all kinds of problems."

"It already has, right? That guy, the Crime Fritzer, tried to apprehend the one stealing from Yolanda's store and he got beat up."

"That's exactly what I'm talking about." He nodded emphatically. "He should have called 911 and let us handle it. As far as I know, he's still in the hospital."

Tally looked in the direction the amateur patrol car had gone. "You're right. He shouldn't have confronted the thief at the broken window. But some of them are doing extra patrols—from their cars—to help out with the...crime wave. That's what they called it."

"They used that term? Crime wave?"

"Yes, and I wondered about that. Is there one? I hadn't heard of it."

He hesitated before answering. "There kind of is, but we haven't publicized it at all. I wonder how they caught wind of that. I'd rather no one talked about that right now." She nodded. "Nothing too major is going on, but a lot of petty theft lately. Just don't get mixed up with them, okay?"

"I don't think I have time to join them, if that's what you mean."

"Partly. There are some things I can't discuss with you, but just promise me you won't have anything more to do with them. Or with trying to find out what's going on, all by yourself."

"My landlady is one of them!"

He shook his head slowly. "I know. I wish she weren't."

Before he left, they set up a tentative lunch date for Monday, Tally's day off.

4

Yolanda knew she was going to be late, but she had to answer the call from Kevin. Things had been running hot and cold between them, bumpy and smooth, lately. When they were cold and bumpy the last time, she made a promise to herself that she would give their relationship every chance she could after he said his divorce was going through. She missed being with Kevin when they were on the outs. Their shops were next door to each other and things could get awkward, at the very least. Although she didn't think of Kevin's winery outlet as a shop. He sold local and imported wines and had tastings regularly. And *awkward* wasn't really the word for how things could get between them. It was much too mild.

"How's it going? You busy right now?"

"Kevin, I have dinner at my parents' place tonight."

"Ah. It's Saturday, isn't it? Sorry. I forgot." Sometimes she wanted to ditch that family dinner tradition. Maybe she'd be that brave one day.

"How about Monday? I'll be crazy busy working during the day and I bet y'all will be, too."

"Yeah, I sure hope so. I need to work in the vineyard on Monday. I haven't spent more than a half an hour at a time there for weeks."

They decided they would try for another day, to be determined, and Yolanda took off for the huge ranch her parents owned at the edge of town.

She drove through the gates at twilight, fireflies blinking in the yard beside the long driveway leading to the large house, made to look deceptively rustic on purpose. The glow of old-fashioned-looking lanterns competed with the fireflies for the last half of the driveway. She could smell the chlorine of the pool before it was in view. She hadn't been in the water yet this year, but maybe she'd bring her bathing suit next Saturday. There weren't any other cars present, so it would be just the three of them, her and her rather old-fashioned parents. Not for the first time, she wondered if she should bring Kevin along one of these Saturday nights.

Her mother called her over to the pool deck and Yolanda accepted a margarita from her father before she curled into a chaise lounge. Yolanda got her dark good looks from both her Italian father and her Latina mother. Luckily, she had avoided her father's thick, bushy eyebrows, but the whole family had the same dark, curly, luxuriant hair and flashing black eyes. Her father was dripping from the swim he had just taken, but her mother, though she wore a bright-red bathing suit, had not been in. Yolanda was in one of her colorful outfits, a long turquoise top with green yoga pants. She usually didn't swim, not wanting to get her thick hair wet, and she hadn't intended to tonight, either.

Her father toweled off and they all sat and talked about the weather. Yolanda was glad he hadn't mentioned her payment. She had half expected him to offer it back to her again.

Before she was halfway through the drink, her father asked her if she would like to invite "that nice Kevin Miller to dinner sometime," as if he had been reading her mind. Most of the local residents knew each other, living in such a small town, but dinner at the house of a woman's parents was a formal step forward, Yolanda knew, to her old-world father. It was a precursor to something she and Kevin had never discussed. Not that Yolanda had never thought about it.

"Oh, I don't know. Maybe sometime. If he's not busy." She kept her voice casual, unenthusiastic, so as not to encourage him to insist on it. She never directly contradicted her father, or said no to him, if she could help it. Experience had taught her that was a bad idea.

"Since you two are seeing each other, Yolie," her mother said, joining in, "we should probably get to know him a little better." Her mother was old-world also, just a nicer version of it.

But should Kevin get to know *them* a little better? That was the question.

"Next Saturday would be perfect." Her father's smile indicated something else was going on.

So she asked. "What would be perfect about next Saturday, Papa?"

He busied himself making her another drink since she had drained hers.

Yolanda wondered if she would need three of them tonight. On the best Saturday, she required two to get through the meal. She looked the question at her mother, who also smiled, but also did not answer her.

Something was going on next Saturday, and she was pretty sure it was something she didn't want to subject Kevin to.

* * * *

Later, after Tally had given Nigel something to eat and they'd had a petting-purring session, she wondered if she should worry about Mrs. Gerg. After all, one of her fellow Fritzers had been badly beaten with a crutch. He was maybe still in the hospital. And Jackson's warning had her worried.

Wait a minute. Her mind whirred as she thrummed her fingers on Nigel's head. He didn't appreciate that and left her lap.

She tried to put some pieces together. The pickup driver in that wreck went to the hospital. With a broken leg. He would most likely have come out of there on crutches the night before the break-in, wouldn't he? Was there a connection with crutches here? She thought about what it would be. The member of the patrol said he was beaten with crutches and, the night before, a man was in a wreck and was put on crutches. And a man on crutches shoved Lily just before Yolanda's theft. Were they all the same man? She didn't see a lot of people hobbling around Fredericksburg on crutches.

She soaked in the bathtub for a luxurious half hour, then snuggled up with Nigel in bed, all the while thinking about everything that was going on. She would definitely avoid actually working with the Crime Fritzers—that would be easy—but she would ask Mrs. Gerg a couple of questions to see if there was a connection. Maybe the man on crutches was the one who stole the plastic and the valuable jade—that is, if Jackson was right about it actually being valuable jade. More information was needed if she was to find out what was going on with their plastic candy. There were a few more pieces of it at Yolanda's place. They hadn't used all of the ones they had ordered. Yolanda had stuck them somewhere. Maybe, for them to ever use the plastic in the future would be altogether too dangerous.

* * * *

When Arlen Snead got the call from Thet Thura, he realized something had gone horribly wrong with this last shipment. He was being summoned to drive up to the warehouse. Before he left, he set his laptop on the counter where the infrequent customers checked out and searched for news from the town of Fredericksburg. He almost missed it, but there it was. A wreck between a Planet Earth truck and a pickup. And one man sent to the hospital. The shipment he'd received from Planet Earth hadn't held any contraband. That wasn't right, but Arlen had decided to wait to be told what to do about it.

He locked up his store, got into the van that had his sign, *Arlen's Aqua Shop*, on the side, and headed to Fredericksburg area to meet his employer. There had been another story on the internet about a man being beaten when a shop window was smashed during a theft. He recognized the name of the shop, Bella's Baskets. It just so happened that he had some kin in that town and visited a couple of times a year.

On his way southwest, to the Hill Country, he talked to Thet on his cell phone. Thet told Arlen that the shipment had been misdirected in Myanmar. He had tried to intercept it, but that went wrong. He wanted Arlen's help finding a man named Walter Wright, who had been mentioned in a news article. He'd been beaten up in front of Bella's Baskets and Thet thought he might have the jade, or might know where it was. The young man he'd hired to divert the shipment, Mateo, had filled him in on some of the details of what happened, but was short on exactly what caused the wreck and prevented them from recovering the merchandise. Mateo was helpful, though. He said Walter Wright was in the local crime watch group and told Thet where he might be now.

* * * *

Four hours later, Thet Thura met Arlen Snead at the small lodging place at the edge of town and Arlen checked into a room down the hall from his. Arlen said he had to get something to eat, so Thet returned to his room to wait for him. There were some things about the Dallas man that annoyed Thet. That gooey brown mess of smelly chewing tobacco he kept in his mouth, and the way he spit it on the ground—that was about the worst thing about him. He was smart, though, and had good ideas. He'd been a help getting this pipeline established. Thet hoped he could help straighten out the problem.

Thet stared at the walls of his musty, none-too-clean room, thinking. Arlen had to help him. They had to figure out what had happened. His uncle, U Win, would disown him if he lost a whole shipment. He would have to leave the family business. If that happened, he had no idea what would happen to him. He walked to the small, dingy lobby and picked up a newspaper from a metal kiosk there. He hoped he wouldn't have to spend too much time at this place, or in Fredericksburg.

The story was there. The name of the shop jumped off the page. Bella's Baskets. There had been a problem there, just as Mateo had told him. The window had been broken and plastic candies stolen. Bella's Baskets. Yes, that's definitely where the shipment had been sent to by mistake. Those were *his* plastics and they held *his* jewels. He read, concentrating on each word, to find out exactly what had happened. The only name mentioned was that of the man Mateo had mentioned, Walter Wright. He had been there. Had he broken the window? It didn't seem like it. Had he taken the goods? That also seemed unlikely, since he had been attacked and the article said he had been trying to stop the thief. But his was the only name mentioned. Arlen could help him contact Walter Wright and try to find out what had happened.

Maybe Walter Wright was in the hospital, since the article said he was injured. Thet asked the sleepy man behind the desk at the motel where the hospital was and collected Arlen to drive there and try to find Walter Wright. He was the only connection Thet had to the missing jade.

The two men returned shortly, frustrated because the hospital wouldn't give out any information to anyone but a relative. Thet didn't think he could lie about that since it was unlikely that Walter Wright looked anything like him. Arlen tried, but they looked at his driver's license and turned him down, too.

Maybe he should see if they could get information from the crime watch group. Organizations like that were always looking for volunteers. They would never suspect who he really was and why he was interested in them....

* * * *

Sunday morning, Raul ran into the shop, returning from a gift basket delivery, breathless. "Miss Yolanda, I just talked to my cousin."

She smiled. "Catch your breath. How is your cousin? Mateo, right? He got that new job a few weeks ago?"

"He did, but he had a problem. You know he was working in a warehouse, loading and driving a delivery truck to Dallas, right?"

"For that new warehouse outside town. I remember. He thought he'd love it since he likes driving." Yolanda snipped off pieces and laid out four different kinds of ribbon for the corporate banquet basket she was trying to get an early start on. "Which should I use?" she asked him.

"For that white wicker basket with the big handle?"

She nodded, picking up one snippet, then another to hold next to the basket. "It's for a real estate company of all women. They wanted something feminine, soft."

"What are you putting in it? Pastels, right?"

"Yes. So should I use yellow, blue, green? Maybe not pink."

"Green. That's the color of spring. And the color of money. Anyway, Mateo's loco. He wouldn't mind driving all day, every day. I'd hate it. But he just got fired."

"Oh no." Yolanda stuck the other spools into the ribbon drawer and kept out the light green. Raul was right, that's what she should use. "What happened?" Her allergies weren't too bad today, but her nose was a tad drippy. She was better off when there weren't lilies around, she thought. She gave her nose a swipe and tossed the tissue into the trash.

"He got in a wreck. It was totally his fault, too. He fell asleep."

"Was anyone injured?"

"He said he hit a pickup and the other driver was hurt. Do you want me to get out the box of plastic grass?"

Yolanda thought this was going to end up with an Easter feel to it, so, sure, they might as well use the plastic grass. "Yes, I'll go ahead and get this one done, as much as I can ahead of time. We don't have any other orders right now. It looks kind of like spring. I think that will be a nice look for them."

Raul worried about his cousin Mateo too much, she thought. He was a grown man, though a young one. The cousin deserved to get fired if he fell asleep and caused a wreck with the company vehicle.

* * * *

Thet Thura got the contact person for that crime watch group from Mateo and did some fast thinking.

"I run a business that could help your organization," he said when he called the contact person. "We would like to offer you free business cards for all of your members."

The woman on the phone, who said her name was Olive, seemed happy about that. "That would be wonderful. I've been thinking we could use something like that. Our budget is very small, however."

"All I need is a list of names and I can get them printed up in a few days. A week at the most."

"How soon can you pick up the list from me?"

"I'm free tonight. Can I meet you somewhere? I'd like to get started on it right away."

Soon, Thet had a list of everyone in the Crime Fritzers. The stupid woman had given him the addresses and phone numbers as well. He sent Arlen Snead to Walter Wright's apartment, but he wasn't there. So Thet had Arlen help him start working his way through the list to find out if anyone knew where Walter Wright was. He had to get his jade back. Soon.

5

Tally got her chance to try to find out more about what the Crime Fritzers were up to when Mrs. Gerg called her at work on Sunday.

"I'm terribly sorry," Mrs. Gerg said, "but I can't come around to collect rent tonight."

That was too bad. Tally was overdue on paying it. Her landlady had been collecting around the first of the month since January and it was now the fifth of June.

Mrs. Gerg continued. "Could you possibly bring it over? After work, I mean. I don't want you to leave work for this."

Tally wouldn't have done that anyway. It was Sunday and weekends were almost always busy. She would close up at 7:00 tonight and usually would go home and decompress. Since the holidays last year, she had been closing on Mondays, so Sunday night was kind of her Friday night.

"I can come over to your house sometime between seven-thirty and eight. Would that be okay?" She felt guilty for being late paying, so she had to accommodate her landlady.

"Oh my, yes. I would appreciate that so much."

But why couldn't she walk to Tally's shop or house? She always walked everywhere.

"Is everything all right?" Mrs. Gerg was extremely ambulatory. In fact, she walked miles every day hunting for yard and garage sale goodies. Tally hoped she wasn't laid up. "Can I bring you anything?"

"I'm all right. I don't need anything. It's just that…I'm taking care of someone and don't want to leave him alone right now. I talked him into letting me take care of him for a while. Until he gets back on his feet. He just got out of the hospital."

Tally was dying to know who she was taking care of, but didn't want to pry, since Mrs. Gerg hadn't offered. Maybe she'd see when she went over there tonight.

Tally observed Molly, trying to tell if she was still feeling down, or if she was in a better mood. She thought the poor young woman was probably overwhelmed by her family situation. She was the only one in her family who was working, after all. She had dropped out of college to come home to help out her parents. Did she want to finish school eventually? Maybe she thought she would never be able to finish. Tally knew that she herself would be impatient, frantic, maybe even depressed, in the same situation

"Are you sure about that?" the customer asked Molly, smiling, looking at the change in his hand.

"I think so," Molly answered. "Let me see."

As Molly stared at the change drawer, the customer spread her change on the counter, saying, "I think you gave me too much." Tally could see two twenties fanned out with some ones and a sprinkling of change.

"Oh. Sorry." Molly scooped up the money and made the right change.

That was a sure sign Molly was distracted, Tally knew. The till came up short on days when Molly wasn't paying attention.

A few minutes later, they were side by side, loading new treats into the glass display cases that had been nearly emptied out.

Tally thought she'd try to sound her out.

"What were you majoring in at school, Molly? I don't think I ever asked you that."

Molly tilted her head at her boss, probably wondering why she wanted to know that. "I was studying for a bachelor's in criminal justice."

Tally paused. "Criminal justice. That's fascinating. Do you want to go into law enforcement?"

Molly shook her head and continued rearranging candy pieces on the tray. "Not really. I was going after a law degree, eventually. But, the way things are going, I might not get past a BA. In fact, I might not get that far."

"Oh, you will. I know you will."

Molly smiled, obviously heartened by her boss's encouragement. It transformed her face. But Tally felt a teensy bit bad about that. This was the employee who couldn't make change when she started, Tally thought, whose work ethic was so poor that she took smoker breaks in the alley way too often. Now that she thought about it, though, Tally hadn't seen Molly smoking or vaping at all for quite some time. Maybe she had given up that bad habit. And no customers had complained about getting shortchanged for ages. Maybe Molly was giving out too much change? Tally thought she would have noticed that happening, though.

"Howie came by last night. We talked."

"Wonderful. Are you dating again?"

"I guess. I missed him a lot."

Later, just before she left work, Tally called Mrs. Gerg, thinking that just because it wasn't herself who needed tending, she *was* tied down nevertheless and might need Tally to bring her something.

"Are you sure you don't want me to run into the grocery store, or the drugstore, and pick up something? You have everything you need?"

She heard Mrs. Gerg let out a soft sigh.

"Anything at all. It's no trouble," Tally said.

"Well, I guess I do need some toilet tissue. And maybe a bottle of dish soap."

"Paper plates?" Tally thought that providing for two might stretch her normal supplies of quite a few things.

"Maybe. And some cups? Those big red ones?"

"Napkins? Paper towels?"

"Oh heavens, I don't want you to go to all that trouble."

"It's no trouble, if you need them."

In the end, Mrs. Gerg gave her an extensive list and promised she would pay her for everything as soon as she got there.

It ended up being six bags full of groceries and supplies. Tally made one trip to the front door from her car at the curb, then Mrs. Gerg came out and helped carry the rest inside. An older man sat on her beige sofa, his head bandaged, one foot in a surgical boot, and his arm in a sling. That arm rested on the doilied sofa arm. The room was filled with evidence of Mrs. Gerg's garage sale collecting. Shelves were filled with shells, boxes, bits of jewelry, stacks of old-looking coins, and much more. When Tally didn't get an introduction to the man, she approached him.

"Hi, I'm Tally Holt, one of Mrs. Gerg's renters."

"Walter Wright," he said, extending his left hand to shake hers, since the sling was on his right arm. A pair of crutches lay next to the sofa.

Realization dawned. "Glad to meet you, Walter. You're Mrs. Gerg's crime watch partner, aren't you?" She was pretty sure that was the name Mrs. Gerg had told her a few weeks ago when she joined the group and started patrolling with them.

"One and the same." He smiled.

"It looks like you've had a bad accident," Tally said.

"You could say that. I met my match."

"Your match? Someone did this to you?" She wanted him to say exactly what had happened.

"I'll be fine. I just need to recuperate for a few days. Candy's taking good care of me." His face crinkled when he looked up and gave Mrs. Gerg a smile.

Candy? Tally made her rent checks out to Candace Gerg. She'd never thought of the woman as a Candy, though. Candy returned Walter's smile with a flirtatious look. Tally pressed her lips together to keep from smiling at them herself. Just because they were senior citizens didn't mean they couldn't flirt. He had to be the Fritzer who was beaten up at Yolanda's the other night. So this is who Mrs. Gerg talked into coming to her house so she could "take care" of him. She was sweet on Walter. Tally pressed her lips tighter to keep from grinning.

"It's the least I can do," Mrs. Gerg said. "He's my partner, after all." She picked up one of the heavy bags, full of canned goods, and headed for the basement door in the kitchen.

"Let me," Tally said. "I can carry those downstairs for you."

"Be very careful on the stairs," Mrs. Gerg said.

Tally lugged two bags down the steep wooden stairs to the dim concrete-floored basement. One wall was lined with shelves that held boxed and canned food. Mrs. Gerg came close behind her.

"See how steep those stairs are? I'm always careful on them."

"I'm impressed with your organization," Tally said, starting to stick the cans onto the shelves.

"Better let me do it," Mrs. Gerg said. "I know where everything goes."

When the goods were neatly stored, they both went up the stairs, Tally behind to make sure Mrs. Gerg didn't fall.

When they got to the living room, and Tally was on her way to the front door, a knock sounded—a loud, impatient knock.

Mrs. Gerg opened the door and a man spoke to her, too softly for Tally to hear. She turned. "Walter? Someone to see you."

Walter Wright jumped up, no longer helpless, apparently, grabbed his crutches and clumped to the door. Two men stood on the porch. Walter flicked on the light and illuminated a tall man and a short one. Tally didn't think Walter recognized either one. The short one was dark and Asian-looking. He wore a nice suit, maybe even silk. The tall, lanky one was all cowboy, the rhinestone type with ostrich boots that had probably never touched a horse, a huge hat, stubbly beard, and bulge of chaw inside his lower lip. Tally hadn't seen anyone use chewing tobacco for a long time.

"I need to speak with you," the shorter man said with a faint accent that Tally couldn't place. He brushed past Walter and came into Mrs. Gerg's house. He was small, slightly overweight and bald. And was brazen, obviously. The taller man followed, more circumspectly, looking around the room.

Mrs. Gerg looked on helplessly, so Tally introduced herself and asked him who he was.

"I am Thet," the short man said. "Thet Thura."

"Happy to meet you," Tally said. "Are you with the crime watchers, too?"

He gave her a brief glance. "I must speak with you," he said again to Walter. "This is about what happened to you. I think I can give you some help. To recover from your injuries."

Tally waited for him to introduce his companion, but he was focused on Walter. "Excuse us." Walter, looking interested, stepped outside with both of the mysterious visitors. She was sure she had never seen either one of them before.

Tally decided to stay inside until their business was concluded, since it seemed to be private. They were only outside a few minutes before Walter came back in. He got around well with the crutches. Tally wondered if he needed them, since he was putting weight on his booted foot.

"Sorry about that," Walter said. "He had a question about…about our crime watch."

Tally wondered why they couldn't talk about that in front of her and Mrs. Gerg. Was there something shady about the crime watch group? Were they connected with the home burglaries?

"They want to join?" Tally asked. "Do they live here?"

Walter shook his head and looked puzzled. "Only the Thura guy spoke to me. Actually, I'm not sure what he wanted. He said he can give me money if I know where something is. Cowwa-something. I don't know what he was talking about."

After Tally paid her rent and left, she realized Walter had never said exactly what had happened to him. He'd met "his match," he said. Was his match a bus, a car, another person? But the paper made it sound like he was beaten at the scene of the robbery. And he did have injuries. Could he be the man on crutches who beat the Crime Fritzer? Whatever it had been, it looked like he was in good hands now.

* * * *

On Monday, Tally's day off, she slept late, or as late as she could with a hungry, insistent cat batting at her nose. She uncurled, rolled onto her back, and stretched.

"Oh, it feels so good to have all the time in the world. For one day, anyway."

Before she could get out of bed, her cell rang.

"Tally?" Jackson said softly. "I have to cancel lunch today."

That was disappointing. But interruptions in schedules were a regular hazard of his job. She knew that.

"See you some other time?" she asked.

"I'll call you tomorrow. Take care." She heard sirens somewhere in the city, racing to the scene of something bad. Maybe Jackson was involved in whatever was going on. Nigel pricked his ears and paid close attention to the noise until it died down.

After she fed Nigel, and then herself, she decided to get dressed and do something she rarely had the chance to do. She set off through her neighborhood, headed for Main Street. True, she walked to work many days, but she was usually concentrating on getting there quickly and going by the most direct route, the same way every day. It would be a luxury to stroll past other people's shops and enjoy her town, pretending to be a leisurely tourist. Maybe meander to some side streets and see what was going on there. The weather was lovely; not too hot yet this early in the day.

She hadn't gone a block on her own street before the sidewalk was clogged with a crowd of her neighbors.

What's going on? she asked herself. Then she saw, through the throng, a police car at the curb. The siren she and Nigel had heard?

"The Schwartzes were robbed," one of her neighbors, a retired farmer, said. "They went out to have an early breakfast this morning and got home to find their back door open."

"What was taken?" Tally asked, trying to remember if she had locked her own back door.

"They're checking," the farmer's wife said. "They think some jewelry and a set of silver are missing."

The Schwartzes were middle-aged schoolteachers with two children in college. This time of year they were probably not going in to work every day. Tally assumed they could ill afford a robbery. But then, who could?

Leaving the scene of the home robbery, she walked west on Austin Street so she could start at one end of Main Street and stroll the whole length of the shops there. The enticing smells of Catfish Haven greeted her as she turned the corner. It was too early for the sidewalks to be crowded yet.

Some of the other shops closed on Mondays, but many stayed open, so the downtown would fill up soon enough. Tally took advantage of the extra space to stop and look at each shop on that side of the street. She thought she would go all the way to Elk Street, then cross over and do the other side of the street, stopping for lunch at midday.

After four blocks she saw a crowd ahead, much like the one she'd seen at the Schwartz house. And like the one that had clustered in front of Bella's Baskets the day the window was smashed. As she got closer, she realized it was one of the winery tasting rooms. At least it wasn't Kevin's place, Bear Mountain Vineyards. Yolanda and Kevin had an on-again, off-again relationship that was now on-again, to Tally's relief. She had to see if it was another break-in and robbery. Part of the crime wave she had heard about?

Sure enough, just like the other morning at Bella's Baskets, shards of glass littered the pavement, and the front window was gaping open. Peering past the shoulders of the gawkers, realizing that she was a gawker herself, she could see that the window display had been emptied out. There were usually lots of bottles of wine, artfully arranged on cloth-draped boxes, and now there were bare boxes, the pieces of cloth wadded on the floor of the window. They must have used bottles with actual wine in them for display. That would be a temptation, more so than empty ones. If anyone could tell the difference.

"What happened?" she asked the people at the edge of the group. Most ignored her. One said he didn't know.

Tally saw a familiar face in the gawking crowd, the young Crime Fritzer, Ira Mann. His long blond hair hung almost to the notebook he was scribbling in. A Crime Fritzer should know about the crime, she figured. She scrunched through the crowd to get next to him.

"What happened? Do you know?"

He looked up, startled before his eyes filled with recognition. "Oh. I know you. You were at another crime scene. The window break at—" he flipped through his pages "—Bella's Baskets, right?"

She nodded. "Yes, my shop is next to that one. Was a rock thrown through this one, too?"

"I can't comment at this time."

"Why not? You didn't see a rock, I guess? Looks like a lot of wine was taken. I suppose the thieves can resell that easily enough. Not like those plastic candies."

He frowned, puzzled.

"That's what was stolen at Yolanda's. At Bella's Baskets."

"It was?" He scanned his notes. "I wasn't informed."

Tally wondered if she was supposed to tell people what was stolen. "I may be mistaken. I assumed, so don't quote me on that."

"I assure you I won't." He sounded so earnest, like he *would* quote her on other subjects. Were all the Crime Fritzers so earnest and meticulous? She pictured meetings of the group where they sat in a circle and took turns standing, reading from their notes and reporting every detail of what happened on their watch.

"Good." She hunched up her shoulders and squeezed her way out of the crowd.

Maybe there actually was a crime wave going on. There was one today, anyway. The Crime Fritzers were on the case, at least on the Main Street case, not the East Schubert Street case. If they actually had stepped up the patrols, it didn't seem to be working to prevent burglaries. Should she be more careful with her own home and her own store? What would she do if Tally's Olde Tyme Sweets got robbed? She had insurance for that, but it would be traumatic, nevertheless. For her and for the others who worked there. It was good anyway that the places getting robbed seemed to get hit only when no one was there. There didn't seem to be a danger to any people, just to their property. And to Walter, who had been there. Just what Detective Rogers warned them about.

She could ask Dorella what was going on. Ira might be telling her more than he was willing to tell Tally right now. On the other hand, the police weren't sharing information with the watch group. Detective Jackson Rogers considered them a nuisance, and Ira hadn't known much about Yolanda's incident, or the present one, either. She could try to get some idea from Jackson of what was going on, if she should be worried or not.

For now, she was determined to carry out her original intent. To enjoy her day off and window-shop to her heart's content.

6

Yolanda woke early on Monday, her day off. Her first thought was of spending the day with Kevin. Then she remembered—Kevin was spending his day off working in his vineyard. The picturesque region around Fredericksburg, known as the Texas Hill Country, held an abundance of vineyards, many with tasting rooms. The town itself boasted about the wineries and the local wines they produced, enticing visitors to try them, even giving organized wine tours.

Kevin liked to get hands-on regularly in his own vineyard to keep track of how his vines were doing and also how his workers were faring. She and Kevin had been spending time together whenever they could, ever since he assured her that his divorce was finally imminent, but she was on her own today.

It was too early to call Tally. She liked to sleep in on her days off. Instead, Yolanda decided to do something for herself. She enjoyed getting in her car, a small, sporty Nissan, and exploring obscure country roads. After a quick bowl of cereal with a sliced banana, she poured coffee into her go-cup and took off. Maybe north today, she thought. She had been too busy to do a random drive like this for a long time, so any direction would do.

To the annoyance of the other drivers, she poked along, enjoying the breeze coming through her open windows and tangling her already unruly long curls. She had thrown on a bright-pink peasant blouse with ruffled sleeves and collar, which the wind played with, too, flipping the collar up onto her face. She laughed at that.

The fresh, pollen-laden air started to affect her sinuses after a short distance, though, and she rolled the windows partway up, reluctant to shut the warm breeze out entirely.

She passed a place where the shoulder was torn up. There were deep, wide tire tracks in the dirt, tracks that had to have been made by a large truck. She wondered if this was where the wreck that Raul's cousin had been in happened, the one that got him fired from the company whose truck he drove to Dallas for deliveries. He'd been driving a large truck, a semi, when he fell asleep at the wheel.

After a few more miles, she saw a sign that hadn't been there the last time she came this way. It proclaimed that Gordon Warehouses was located down the next road to the right. A few more company names were below that one on the sign. Yolanda thought they were probably businesses that used the warehouses for storage. One was Planet Earth Plastics.

Yolanda would be the first to admit that she didn't keep up with local news, but she was, nevertheless, surprised that a big new enterprise was located right outside her town and she hadn't heard of it.

Curious, she turned down the dirt road, quickly rolling up her windows against the dust her tires kicked up. Soon, after a fairly intense sneezing fit from the dust, she came upon a drab metal prefab warehouse building, about as big as two or three large barns. A paved parking lot held a couple dozen cars and, on one side, two large trucks stood at loading bays whose doors were closed. Everything appeared gray, neutral, and there were no people around. One of the trucks backed up to the loading dock had a dent in the front grille. Probably not enough to affect its drivability. Was this the truck from the wreck? *Raul's cousin Mateo must work for this company.*

She pulled into the parking lot and turned around. As she was driving away, pieces of the puzzle began to fall into place in her mind. She took one more glance at the sign again and noticed the Planet Earth Plastics name again.

It wasn't until she was back on the highway again that she put the whole picture together and realized this might be the warehouse where their molded candies had been stored. And was it the company Raul's cousin Mateo had worked for? Had she heard Raul, or someone, mention the name? She tried to dredge that up. Then she realized she could picture the box they had been packed in when they arrived. Yes, the box proclaimed to be Planet Earth Plastics. There was a motto on the carton that said something about saving the planet. She should probably remember the company better, but she hadn't ordered the products. Just received and displayed them. And had them stolen.

She drove on, away from town, until she was almost to Kevin's vineyard. Not wanting to bother him there, she turned around before she reached it, and came back. When she got into Fredericksburg, she would call Tally and see if she wanted to have lunch.

* * * *

Thet Thura hadn't found his jewels yet. Walter didn't know anything about them. But he must know someone who did. The man was there when they had been stolen from Bella's Baskets.

Arlen Snead said he wanted to take a ride around town, had some business to attend to, so he took off in the van from the aquarium shop that he had driven up from Dallas.

Thet's uncle called from Myanmar asking him when he was going to recover them. The phone call made Thet sweat, even though the temperatures in this part of Texas were much cooler than those in Myanmar, where he had been only a few days ago. When U Win demanded results, he got them. If he didn't, that was very bad news for the person who disappointed him. Thet knew that at least two of his cousins, who had disappeared after letting their uncle down, were no longer among the living. No one would ever find their bodies, but Thet knew what had happened to them, anyway.

The last thing he wanted was to disappoint U Win. The next to the last thing was to face him right now, before he had any answers. Nevertheless, the man had told him that he was on his way to the States. Thet imagined him shutting off the phone and stepping onto a plane immediately. He had to find the jade.

He would go visit Walter Wright again as soon as he could. He called Arlen, wanting him to come along, but there was no answer. So Thet left his motel room and headed to the newspaper stand that sat in the lobby. He put coins in the slot and bought one, hoping there was something in it that would help him.

Thet perched on a plastic couch to thumb through the paper. His concentration in reading the strange language was broken by an argument at the desk.

"That doesn't do any good. I turned it up. It's still too hot in my room." The young man's voice was strident.

A calmer voice answered. "I can't get anyone to fix it right this minute. Give me an hour and I'll have someone look into it. I'm sure we can cool your room down."

Thet looked up and the angry young man turned from the desk and went to the elevators. He was on crutches. Perhaps he was the person Mateo had asked to help with the hijacking. That person had gotten his leg broken and this young man was on crutches. What was he doing here? In this motel? Surely he lived somewhere close by. Was he hiding? Why would that be?

Thet narrowed his eyes in anger. He realized that the man on crutches might have the contraband. He might have taken it from Bella's Baskets. Thet needed to find out what room he was staying in. Could the jade be this close to him?

* * * *

Tally grabbed a salad at a small café with outdoor seating. She was having such a restful day off, away from the recent troubles, emptying her mind—or trying to. It was lovely sitting under the awning in the shade, watching the noisy crowds amble past. Some were laden with purchases, she was happy to see. If people bought from one store, they were likely to buy from the others, she figured. The local businesses all rose or fell together. She took a bite of her salad. It was cool and crisp and the dressing just tangy enough, served on the side so she could avoid drowning her salad. The croutons were even delectable, small and herbed to perfection.

As she was finishing, spearing the last crisp morsels of lettuce, Mrs. Gerg walked by. Tally called to her, asking if she wanted to join her. She could always get another glass of iced tea to stay and keep her company. She had the whole day off.

"Oh, Tally, I can't today. I'm getting lunch for my dear Walter and bringing it back."

Her *dear Walter*? "Is he still staying with you today?"

"Oh my, yes. He can't be alone yet. He has so much trouble getting around, doing things, you know."

Tally nodded. He did have a broken leg, or foot, or something. Even though it didn't seem to impede his movement much. "He doesn't have family to take care of him?"

Mrs. Gerg ducked her head and giggled. "He much prefers my company."

"What about his friends?"

"Friends?"

"You know, those two guys who came over when I was there. Tut—no, it's Thet, right? Did you ever learn the name of the other one, the tall guy with the cowboy hat?"

"He's Arlen Snead, Walter said. They're from out of town. I don't think they're friends of Walter's, more like acquaintances. They do some sort of business together. I think."

"What business is Walter in?" Tally asked.

That question flustered Mrs. Gerg. Candy. "I don't really know. He doesn't talk about it. I didn't know him very well before Crime Watch. Isn't it nice we got assigned to do our routes together? He just has to not go alone and on foot anymore."

"How much longer will you need to tend him, do you think? Could he go to a rehab place?" Poor Mrs. Gerg, being tied down by an invalid she didn't know anything about and wasn't even related to.

She stared at Tally. "Oh my, no. I wouldn't want that. I like having…a man in the house. Especially this one."

"Are you…?" Tally wasn't sure how to phrase it, but Mrs. Gerg's bright eyes made her look like a teenager with a crush. Definitely not like an older woman tied down by an unwelcome disabled guest.

Mrs. Gerg leaned over the short railing and spoke softly. "Tally, I think I'm growing very fond of him. And him of me, of course. I wouldn't mind if he moved in." She nearly simpered.

"Mrs. Gerg, be careful." Tally was alarmed. "Do you know enough about him?"

She turned her head and cut her eyes, giving Tally a knowing look. "I know all I need to know."

"Have the other men been back?" Tally had gotten a bad feeling about them, even beyond what was warranted by Thet's rudeness, barging in like he did. It was suspicious he had wanted to talk about crime watch, but not in front of another crime watch member.

"No, no. The one called, though. He was being so brave, Walter was."

"Brave? When?"

"When that thief beat him up with his crutches."

"Was he the person who apprehended our thief? Tried to, I mean?"

Mrs. Gerg gave a sorrowful sigh. "Yes, he was trying to catch him. He's a hero, really."

A foolish one, Tally thought. Patrolling alone and on foot, which they had been advised not to do by the police. She wished she knew more about the mysterious men on Mrs. Gerg's porch, too. Something about them put her on alert the minute she saw them. Maybe she could learn more about them from Walter.

Watching Mrs. Gerg cross the patio and enter the café to order, Tally thought to herself, *That woman is smitten.* It was cute, but Tally couldn't help but be uneasy about it. Older women made such easy targets. Age seemed to project vulnerability. And too many people in the world took advantage of it.

That evening, she would be spending even more time with older women, as she was paying her more-or-less weekly call on the local nursing home, Setting Sun Home. She had started visiting there from a sense of obligation a few months ago and now continued because of several factors.

The first, a selfish reason, was that these visits made her feel good about herself, like she was doing a good thing. Many of the residents had outlived their friends and families and they had no one left who either could or wanted to come see them. Her heart always felt warmer after she'd been there, helping out.

The second reason was that the staff let her know, every time she showed up, that they appreciated her help as a volunteer. There was always plenty for her to do and much of it lightened the burden of those who worked there. So she felt welcome by the staff every time she went.

Thirdly, she knew that the residents counted on her stopping to chat, to read to them, to make them more comfortable by shifting their weight or their pillows when they couldn't do it for themselves. She also fed them in the dining room when she was there at their dinnertime, and helped walk or wheel them to and from the meal. That made her feel needed, on top of all the other good feelings.

She couldn't quit coming to Setting Sun now, even if she wanted to. She left the place this day, as always, with a feeling of a job well done and a sense of accomplishment.

Later, before she climbed into bed, Tally stuck her phone onto the charger. The screen brightened and that's when she saw she'd missed a couple of calls from Yolanda. She must have not heard her phone while she was making her way through the ever-increasing crowds on her shopping spree. She had netted a new pair of sandals and two sleeveless tops, so it had been a good day. Of course, she had tried on a dozen pair of shoes and two dozen tops that she didn't buy, but she always considered it a success when she came home with anything.

She called Yolanda, hoping it wasn't too late.

"Did you see my texts?" Yolanda asked, yawning. "I just took an antihistamine. I'm conking out."

No, she hadn't seen those texts, either. She might as well have left her phone at home. "What did I miss?"

"Only the opportunity to have lunch with me, you poor thing."

"Oh, sorry, Yo. I would have liked that. I was just messing around, shopping."

They discussed, in detail, what Tally had purchased. She could hear Yolanda yawning.

"You're falling asleep in my ear."

"I'll tell you about my drive when I can hold my head up and my eyes open," Yolanda said.

Then Tally conked out, too, wanting a full night's sleep before her workday tomorrow.

* * * *

Thet, with the help of Arlen, had partly accomplished what he needed to do. Now he needed a place to hide the treasure so it wouldn't be found until he could bring it to Dallas. He thought of the accommodating Walter Wright, crippled and on crutches, and of the old woman he was staying with. They were two people he could easily manage. He and Arlen called on them again around noon.

* * * *

Jackson Rogers called Tally midmorning and asked if she wanted dinner with him after work. Of course she did. What a silly question.

However, after she happily spent the day in an extra-sunny mood, looking forward to seeing him, he called again, midafternoon. She knew before he began speaking to her that it was probably bad news for their dinner. That was the nature of his job.

"Sorry Tally, gotta work a homicide. I won't be able to get away for dinner."

"Someone was *murdered*!?" Tally shuddered. So many bad things seemed to be piling up in Fredericksburg. "Who was it?"

"You know I can't talk about this. Yet. But it's no one you would know."

That was a relief. It was probably crazy, but her first panicked thought had been for Mrs. Gerg. It seemed so strange that Walter Wright had moved in with her. Tally knew nothing about him and didn't think Mrs. Gerg did, either. The whole situation gave her a bad feeling. She might as well mention it to Jackson. He might tell her something reassuring.

"You know, I'm a little worried about Mrs. Gerg." He probably couldn't do anything about it, but she had to try. "Do you know anything about the man who's staying with her? He's her crime watch partner. He's also the person who got beat up in front of Yolanda's."

"I can't do anything today, but I can check him out later for you if you'd like. Remind me of his name again."

"Walter Wright. I think he's lived in Fredericksburg for a little while—I mean, he must have, being on the crime watch and all, but I've never seen him before." The town population was less than 12,000, but Tally hadn't been living there long enough to get to know everyone. "Do you know him?"

"Yes, I remember. The Crime Fritzer. I know a little about him. He's a strange dude. Parents are dead, never married, no kids, no relatives that I know of."

"Strange how?"

"Unsettled. He doesn't get into any real trouble, but I always wonder if that's just because he hasn't ever been caught. He doesn't have any arrest record. He's always kind of drifted from job to job. For a stretch, he was homeless. He's done ranch work, restaurant work, even a janitor at the old folks' home. I don't know what he's doing now. He might still be there."

"I don't think he's working at the home. I haven't seen him since I started volunteering there."

After she hung up she felt a tiny bit better about Mrs. Gerg. At least Jackson knew something about Walter Wright. If he'd been bad news, had been in trouble with the law, he would have mentioned that.

7

Yolanda got a call from her sister, Violetta, as she was leaving for the day, but waited until she got home to her quaint Sunday House to return it.

"Vi? How is everything?" They hadn't spoken in over a week. Yolanda felt she had to keep in better contact with Violetta now since their parents had, in general, cut off communication with their younger daughter recently.

"We're doing great." She sounded happy. "Eden and I are going to the newest restaurant in Dallas tonight."

"What kind of food?" Being part Italian, the whole Bella family was interested in food.

"Afghan. I have no idea what the food is like, but the reviews are terrific and a couple people from the office have gone and loved it."

"I'm jealous," Yolanda said, kicking off her shoes and curling up on her brocade couch. It was an unlikely spot for her to be comfortable, since it was rather stiff and hard, but Yolanda managed it. "Tell me about it later, okay?"

"Maybe I'll take you there if you ever come and see us."

It had been too long since Yolanda had gone to Dallas and her sister rarely came to Fredericksburg any more, since she wasn't welcome at their parents' house after she had come out of the closet and introduced them to her girlfriend, Eden.

"I promise I'll come see y'all," Yolanda said. "Soon."

They said their goodbyes and hung up, but Yolanda wondered how she was going to manage a trip to Dallas. Vi got weekends off and she took off Mondays. Someday soon she would have to close up for a couple of days and just do it. Her sister should have at least some family support, and Yolanda dearly loved her.

Tonight, though, she was also going out to dinner. With Kevin. She set a timer for a ten-minute nap. After she roused from that, refreshed, she changed her clothes, donning a blue-and-aqua caftan and a necklace of large pink stones. Her hands were not quite steady, thinking about their upcoming meeting. Kevin had said he had some big news and she was a bit nervous about that. She hadn't been able to tell, over the cell phone, whether this was going to be good news or bad news.

They met at the Auslander. Yolanda found a lucky parking place by the front door and entered the Bavarian restaurant, greeted by a loud band echoing off the hard tile floor. The band that was playing, Stomping Grapes, was one of her favorite local bands, but tonight she wanted to be able to converse with Kevin in peace.

The place was packed and she wondered if they'd even be able to get a table. To her relief, she scanned the place for only a few seconds before spotting Kevin on a stool at the bar. The smile he greeted her with relaxed her somewhat. Maybe his news was the good variety.

Then something else occurred to her. What would constitute good news? Was he going to propose? He wasn't especially dressed up, clad entirely in black, as usual—black jeans, shirt, boots—to match his black perennially-three-day-old beard. She loved his look, the opposite of her flamboyant taste in fashion. They were foils for each other. She'd never seen him dressed any other way, except when he was toiling in his vineyard in shorts and an undershirt. That wasn't a bad look for him, either.

He hopped off the stool, carrying his beer. Putting his mouth close to her ear so he didn't have to shout, he asked, "Do you want to sit outside? It's quieter."

She nodded and Kevin gave a signal to the hostess, who led the way to an empty table for two under the open latticework covering. Yolanda gratefully took a seat, glad that they'd be able to talk here. The band music was fainter, but still sounded good from their table.

She ordered a glass of white wine. Kevin liked to take a break from wine sometimes and tonight was one of them. The waiter brought him a new stein when he delivered her stemmed glass of Chardonnay. After they ordered their dinners, Yolanda waited, expectantly, for the news.

"Anything new going on with you?" he asked.

Okay, he was going to delay. "Not much, just still dealing with the aftermath of what Tally calls the Broken Window Incident. Did y'all hear about the wreck outside town? I drove out to where the accident happened."

"I did. It's on the way to my fields, I think. But how did you know where it was?"

"I could tell. The ground is plowed up. That new warehouse isn't very far from there."

"Warehouse?"

"The one our plastic was shipped from. The stuff that got stolen from my window display."

Kevin sipped his beer. "I've seen the building, too. Gordon Warehouses. It just popped up there not too long ago. I wondered what they did. There's a sign that says Planet Earth, too, right?"

She couldn't wait any longer. "Okay, what is it you have to tell me? You said you had news."

He grinned. "I do. Good news. Rachel agreed to everything."

Rachel?

"You don't know who Rachel is, do you? She's my wife. My *ex*-wife. It's all done."

Yolanda realized she had never heard the woman's name. Kevin always referred to her as "my wife."

"The divorce went through?" Yolanda gaped. She sometimes thought it would never happen. It had been years in the making. "You're free?"

"Yes. Finally. She met someone in Amarillo and decided to stop torturing me. I'm a free man."

He raised his stein and Yolanda clinked her wineglass against it. "Congratulations! That *is* good news."

"I really think we're both happy about it."

"You worked long and hard for this. Are we celebrating tonight?"

"Sure. Let's get something wonderful for dessert."

They both hurried through their meals and dug into a huge serving of apple strudel, complete with sugared dates and toasted pecans and topped with whipped cream and caramel.

Kevin walked her out, both of them talking about how they were about to burst. Yolanda was also elated about Kevin's long, contentious battle finally being over. She knew it had preyed on his mind for a long time.

Yolanda unlocked her car and opened the door. Kevin took hold of the door. She expected him to lean over and kiss her, but his face got a clouded look.

"There's just one person unhappy about our split," he said.

Yolanda waited, holding her breath. Bad news on top of the good news?

"Kaycee."

Another woman whose name she had never heard. She raised her eyebrows.

He looked at the ground. "Our daughter. She's upset about it. I don't know why. She always knew it would happen." Then he leaned in and kissed her. "Anyway, good night. See you tomorrow."

"Most likely," she said, getting into the car. As she drove away she thought: *Rachel? Kaycee?* She had never heard their names before. She had never even pictured him as a father. What kind of a father was Kevin, she wondered? Did he treat his daughter as her own father treated her? Or maybe nicer, as her father used to treat Violetta? She wondered how old Kaycee was and hoped she was younger than herself. There was a significant age difference between her and Kevin, after all.

* * * *

Thet drove to the tiny county airport to pick up his uncle. He knew the man would not be in a good mood. The flight from Katmandu was very long and tiring. Thet made it often and it wrung him out every time. His uncle was older, so he should be even more affected.

U Win waited until they were in Thet's car before starting to berate him. Thet was glad Arlen wasn't there to witness his scolding. Arlen had said he had some Snead relatives he wanted to call on as long as he was in the area.

"Are there any mistakes you have not made?" Once he started speaking, the older man didn't seem worn out from the trip. He was fresh and full of energy.

"I am so sorry, Uncle. I had a plan, but—"

"You did not have a good plan. If you had a good plan, you would have retrieved our stones."

"Yes, Uncle. That is true." His uncle did not look at him, but kept his eyes straight ahead on the dark road. "I have found them now."

"Let me see them."

"I will. They are not with me."

"Where are they? When can I see them?"

Thet relaxed a notch. His uncle had not struck him. "They are in a safe place. I will take you to the motel now."

"And that is where they are? In a motel? Is that wise? We can take them to Dallas now?"

"No, they are someplace else." Thet's hands started to sweat on the steering wheel. Maybe leaving them at the old woman's house had not been a good plan. "I was afraid my room at the motel might be searched." He didn't want to mention the death at the motel. His uncle would certainly blame him for that immediately.

Now Win turned in his seat and faced Thet with cold, hard eyes. "Why would your room be searched? What else have you done?"

* * * *

Tally had decided she needed to attend a crime watch meeting, for the sake of Mrs. Gerg. Maybe she could settle in her mind whether they were a bunch of people trying to protect everyone's property, or whether they were a front for housebreaking and stealing.

They had a website, very plain, but easy to find since there wasn't anything else named Crime Fritzers. They met at the home of a woman named Olive Baum. The address was residential, so Tally figured they must be meeting in the homes of the members. It wasn't far, and the evening was lovely, so she walked, timing her arrival for a few minutes before the meeting started at eight o'clock.

A hand-lettered sign in the front yard proclaimed, *Meeting here, 8 PM.* Tally wondered if they rotated the locations. The house was a small ranch, similar to her own, with a front porch extending halfway across the front. Sturdy posts held up the porch roof, brick on the bottom half, white-painted wood on the top of the columns. The front yard had a bit of grass as well as some bare dirt. A beautiful yard was not the focus of Olive Baum.

Tally stepped up onto the porch. The view through the screen door showed that the inside door stood open. She guessed they weren't too worried about security since all the patrol teams would be here.

Tally found herself in a crowded living room, not with people, but with furniture. Two full-sized couches took up half the room, and several other upholstered chairs were crammed into the spaces beside them. Folding chairs took up a lot of the remaining floor space.

A short, thin, dark-haired woman holding a clipboard jerked her head up when Tally entered.

"Who are you?" She sounded rude, but maybe she was taken aback by a stranger, Tally thought.

"Hi. My name is Tally Holt."

"Do you live here?"

"Well, in Fredericksburg, yes. A few streets over. I wanted to come and check out the group and see—"

"Check us out for what?" Her abrupt, clipped tone continued, not softening one little bit.

Tally was tempted to say, "For lice." But she smiled, a futile attempt. The woman frowned in return. "I'm interested in the group." She didn't want to lie and say she wanted to join, but she wanted the woman to assume that.

"We don't need any more members." The woman turned her back on Tally.

Two other people were in the room, both middle-aged men. They were following the exchange, swiveling their heads like they were watching a tennis match.

"Are you sure?" Tally said. "I know you have two who are not participating right now. Candace Gerg and Walter Wright."

The woman whipped around and faced Tally. "They'll be back."

Tally was growing angry at the rude woman and decided to call her bluff. "I'll just stay for the meeting, in case." She plopped down into one of the large stuffed chairs, figuring she would be hard to dislodge from there.

One of the men smiled, amused at the whole thing, she thought. He approached her and stuck his hand out. "Hi, I'm Kyle Meyer."

Tally shook his hand, recognizing that smoker's rasp in his voice. She remembered the balding, beer-bellied man. He had been with Ira Mann when she met him in front of Yolanda's shop right after her window got fixed. They had said they were on patrol, but their car hadn't been marked with a magnetic sign like the others that she saw.

"Hi," she said. "You're Ira's partner, right?"

The smile left his face for a fleeing moment. "Well, sort of. I'm officially partnered with Ray, here." He gestured to the other man in the room, a middle-ager of similar build and age. Ray threw her a smile and a salute.

The room eventually filled up with crime watchers and every seat was taken. The temperature grew uncomfortable with all the bodies jammed into the small space. It was loud, too, with some people conversing across the room, others to the people next to them.

"Okay, the meeting shall come to order," Olive announced, a surprisingly large voice coming from her small frame. The room grew quiet, but was still very hot.

"Report from Team One," Olive yelled.

Her request was met with silence. "Team One," she said, louder.

A nice-looking gray-haired woman answered. "We don't have any report."

"You have to report something," insisted Olive.

"Well, we drove our patrol. Nothing happened."

Olive frowned at the poor woman, but wrote something down on her clipboard.

"Team Two. Report in."

"All quiet on our shift," Kyle said. Ray, sitting next to him, nodded.

This went on until, apparently, all the teams had reported in. No one had anything to report. Tally thought it might have been more efficient if she had asked if anyone actually had a report.

"People," Olive shouted. "We have to be more vigilant. Crimes are being committed and we're missing them."

A young woman sitting across from Tally dared to answer her. "We can't be on patrol all the time, Olive. It's a matter of chance, catching anyone doing a crime. Besides, they can see us coming."

"Aren't we supposed to be a deterrent?" Ray, Kyle's partner, asked. "The police don't really want us apprehending criminals. Just being there to let them know...well...that we're there."

Olive shot out an impatient breath. "That's not good enough. We *can* catch them. We must try harder."

Tally saw, from the blank faces in the room, that they had no idea how to go about trying harder. They drove their patrol routes, she thought. What else could they do? She knew the police didn't want them catching criminals, as Olive had suggested.

"What are you saying?" asked the woman across from Tally. "Do more patrols? Recruit more members?"

Olive glanced at Tally before she answered. Tally smiled at her, just to disconcert the woman. She had told Tally they didn't need more members, but her words were implying that they did.

"Just be more vigilant! Do your jobs! Meeting adjourned." Olive whacked her pen on her clipboard. Tally wondered if she really wanted a gavel.

"Where is the next meeting?" Tally asked.

"We meet here," Olive snapped, and left the room, leaving everyone to make their way out.

Tally overheard one man muttering to another one, "I told you not to make her president. Remember? I told you."

The other man shook his head. "Yes, you did."

Tally left, thinking that the Crime Fritzers probably didn't have much of a future with that unpopular, prickly woman running it. Halfway back to her house, Tally realized that Ira Mann hadn't been there. He hadn't been called on for a report, either. Kyle had been evasive about being his partner. Was Ira a real Crime Fritzer? It didn't seem like he was, not officially, as Ray put it.

* * * *

On Wednesday morning, another fine sunshiny day, Tally got up early enough to have a leisurely breakfast, and even cooked herself some eggs. Nigel liked a few little bits of egg mixed with bacon, so she would sometimes put them into his bowl, but he never considered the portion adequate. She gave him just a tad more, then lectured him about his weight, which he didn't appreciate. He stalked off into the living room mid-lecture after he had finished off the paltry meal.

"Okay, be that way. Bye now. I have to go to work."

Nigel did not relent or forgive her before she gave a shrug and went out the door.

She took her time walking to work, enjoying the colorful spring bulbs in her neighbors' yards, daffodils, narcissus, and some tulips just starting to open. One neighbor had a densely planted flower bed of annuals next to the sidewalk. It rioted with colors: yellow and blue with splashes of red and pink.

On the main street, she paused when a newspaper headline in a metal dispenser caught her eye.

MURDER OF MYSTERY MAN IN MOTEL 11

She frowned. Did she know where Motel 11 was? This must be the homicide that had kept Jackson busy last night. Homicides weren't daily occurrences in this town, so it had to be the same one.

Tally put her money into the slot of the machine and pulled out today's edition of the *Fredericksburg Standard*. The article was short and without many details, except that a man had been found beaten to death in the room he was renting at the Motel 11, at the edge of town, that he had paid cash for the room and no one there knew who he was, and that a pair of crutches found in the room were thought to be the murder weapon.

Crutches again! They were popping up all over the place, Tally thought. There had been that onlooker using them when they had been admiring the Bella's Baskets window display. A window display that was later wrecked by…a man on crutches. They knew about that because Walter Wright had been beaten by that thief with those crutches. Did that same person kill this man at the motel? And was he the same person injured in the bad wreck that Raul's cousin was involved in? The injured motorist, they'd said, had maybe broken his leg.

She wandered down the sidewalk, reading the article a second time, trying to squeeze more details out of the few, sparse words. When she passed Bella's Baskets, Yolanda ran out to flag Tally down.

"Tally, did you hear?"

Tally looked up from the newspaper.

"Come in here for a sec. You have to hear this. Raul's cousin found a dead guy."

"This dead guy?" Tally showed her the headline. "The one in the motel?"

Yolanda squinted at the paper. "I think it must be."

Tally followed Yolanda into the shop where Raul was on a ladder, getting baskets from a high cupboard.

"Raul, tell her," Yolanda said.

"About Mateo?"

Yolanda nodded and Raul jumped down from the ladder, bubbling and eager to spread his news. "My cousin lost his job driving trucks for that warehouse when he was in a wreck, so he started delivering pizzas, and yesterday he got a call for a delivery to that motel out there, the cheap, crummy one."

"Motel Eleven?" Tally asked.

"That's the one." Raul's dark eyes gleamed with the importance and excitement of his news. "So he goes to the door for the room number they gave him and he smells something terrible. He pushes the door open an inch. Doesn't even go in. Gets the manager and the manager calls the cops. Then, when the cops come, they make him stay in the office and miss the rest of his shift. That one policeman was there. The one that's your friend, Ms. Tally."

"Detective Rogers?"

He nodded. "That one. So they just ask Mateo some questions and send him away, after waiting all that time. He doesn't even know there's a dead guy in there until he sees it on the news last night." He had talked so rapidly he was panting, breathless. "But he told me how bad it smelled. And dead bodies don't smell good, right?"

In this weather, it wouldn't take too long for a stench to build up. Tally felt like invisible lines were being drawn, cords that were being tightened between all these events, but she couldn't tell what they meant. Or even where they were. Going from? Going to? All of these elements had to be connected, though.

After she left Yolanda's shop and before she entered her own, she called Jackson from the sidewalk to see if he could have dinner tonight. Maybe he could tell her what was going on. She leaned against the warm outside wall of her shop, beside the display window, out of the way of foot traffic, to call. He didn't answer his phone so she texted him, hoping to hear back before dinnertime.

It would soon be time to open. Dorella Diggs and Molly were inside. Lily came in from the back as Tally entered the front door, setting off the chime. Molly looked up from inspecting Dorella's left hand. Tally caught a flash of sparkle and brightened. Dorella was engaged!

"Look what Ira got her," Molly said, holding up Dorella's hand as if she couldn't do it herself.

No, it wasn't an engagement ring. Unless he bought it way too small, since it was on her pinkie.

Tally came close and looked as Lily joined them. The stone was as large as it could be for a pinkie ring, and a brilliant pink.

"What is it?" Tally asked. "Do you know what the stone is?"

"Ira said it's a pink sapphire," Dorella said. "I looked it up. I think it's worth a lot of money."

"What does Ira do, again?" asked Lily, tilting her head, looking skeptical.

"He's the new fire chief's son," Dorella said. "He...works for him. I think. Sorta. He does odd jobs for the department. He does the crime watch, too."

"I think his daddy is overpaying him," Lily said, tying on her smock and setting up the cash drawer. She chose a lilac one from the pegs that held the pink and lilac aprons.

Dorella shrugged. "I think Ira just likes me." She held her hand up and twisted her wrist so the stone caught the daylight streaming in from the front windows and splayed bright spots of reflection across the walls and ceiling.

"I wouldn't mind if Howie gave me one like that," Molly said, a wistful smile on her face. She ran her left hand through her short, dark hair, maybe wishing there was a ring on one of her fingers, Tally thought.

"It's beautiful," Tally said, thinking it was kind of mean for Lily to be so unenthusiastic, and so critical of Ira. But Tally was thinking the same thoughts, too. Ira Mann didn't seem to have a job that she could see. She had heard the past fire chiefs of the town didn't make an overly robust amount of money, so they often had another job, too. The new chief, Armand Mann, had bought a local ranch, but did so much volunteer work, Tally assumed he was wealthy enough he didn't have to worry about making a living. She knew that Dorella had to work for everything she got, when her biggest desire was to spend time on her art. She was a talented potter, but, like almost all artistic endeavors, making pots didn't bring in a lot of money. She was currently working at Burger Kitchen and Tally's place, as well as another part-time job, doing home health care for a family with an elderly relative on the weekends, relieving the regular weekday caregiver. She wondered how this pair got along, the entitled playboy and the hardworking young woman. And if it would continue long enough for him to put a real engagement ring on her left hand.

8

Lily's bad mood continued and she even snapped at a customer who said she thought their products were unhealthy.

"They're candy," Lily said with a sneer. "How healthy can candy be? Go to a grocery store if you want vegetables."

After the customer left, without buying anything, Tally took Lily to the kitchen. She led her to the upholstered chair Tally had put in the corner to use for breaks and ordered her to sit. She wondered if there was trouble between her and Raul already. As far as Tally knew, they had just started noticing each other.

Before she started asking the young woman what was wrong, Lily volunteered.

"I really like Amy. We've always gotten along well. I thought it would be easy living with her." She sat slumped in the chair, looking dejected and small.

"But it's not?" Lily hadn't been living with her cousin for very long, Tally knew.

Lily looked miserable. "I don't know if it's her or me. Ever since I started seeing Raul, she's been making fun of me."

"How do you mean?"

"She says things like, 'You're not going to wear that, are you?' And 'Maybe you should get a new hairdresser,' right after I got my last cut."

Tally thought Lily always looked darling. Was Amy jealous? "She wasn't that way before you started seeing Raul?"

"No. Never."

"Is she seeing anyone?"

Lily's eyes flew wide open and she sat straight up. "That's it. She was. She was dating the same guy she dated ever since high school. They broke up."

"At the same time she started being hard to get along with?"

"Yes." Lily jumped up from the cushy chair. "I'm so stupid. I should have figured that out."

"She's jealous," Tally said. "You have a boyfriend and she doesn't. Do you think that's bothering her?"

"Yes, she's jealous. That's it. And I've been so upset wondering why we're not getting along. I'm sorry I've been so nasty today."

"Not all that nasty. Just…"

"Yeah, I was. I'll apologize to Dorella."

"So everything is okay between you and Raul?"

Lily widened her large brown eyes. "I think so. We just don't know how it'll go, so we're taking it slow."

Tally nodded in approval. "That's a very good idea. I approve wholeheartedly."

Lily grew more serious. "That means a lot to me. It really does. I think I could get so I like Raul very much."

Wednesday evening, closing time at the shop, finally arrived, after a hard day with, for some reason, a slew of difficult customers, in addition to the drama with Dorella and Lily. That calmed down eventually and they worked together in a tacit truce. However, a couple of the customers argued with Tally about her ingredients, not believing they contained what she said they did. They were essentially calling Tally a liar and it got her back up. It was all she could do to keep smiling at them as they left without buying anything. One young woman insisted on tasting everything in the whole shop. She had gotten about a quarter of the way through the wares before Tally caught on and told her to leave the store if she couldn't make up her mind by now. Tally had lost her smile for that one. Yet another problem arose when a patron bought a bag full of individual candies, left them in her car for two hours, she said, then returned and wanted replacement or a refund because the chocolate had all melted. No. Just no. No refund and definitely no smile. Her head was splitting by then as she polished the glass cases so they would gleam in the morning.

Tally felt her tension headache lifting as she walked to meet Jackson for dinner, having left Molly and Lily to clean up and close up. Molly had made the correct change all day, but Tally should probably still sit down with her again to make sure she was doing okay.

* * * *

They both started on queso and chips with a light, crisp white wine for Tally and beer for Jackson. He asked the server to come back later for their orders, signaling a leisurely evening, to Tally's delight. She could sit in this patio, under the small white sparkle lights strung above, feeling the zephyr like a cool breath on her cheek, and basking in the company of Detective Jackson Rogers. His gray eyes were dark in the twilight, almost black. She felt the headache float away with a sigh of relief.

"How's your friend Yolanda doing?" he asked. "Is she back together with Kevin?" He'd been her sounding board when they had their recent problems.

"I think so. I think they'll be okay. I'm not so sure about her sister, though."

"Oh? What's going on there?"

"The Bellas aren't comfortable with their daughter being gay."

Jackson shook his head. "I gathered that. Violetta is such a sweet kid. That's a shame. Maybe they just need some time to adjust."

"I hope you're right." Tally hoped so, too, but wasn't optimistic about the chances of their father accepting his gay daughter and Eden, the love of Violetta's life. The young women lived in Dallas, hours away by car, so could easily avoid having to deal with the elder Bellas for at least the near future.

"Anyway," Tally said, "Yolanda's place is all repaired from the damage."

Jackson took a swing of beer and a scoop of queso before starting a new topic. "You asked me to watch out for Mrs. Gerg, with Walter Wright moving in. I'm sending a car down her street a couple of times a day. It's strange not to see her walking all over the town like she usually does."

Tally laughed. "Yes, looking for garage and yard sale junk to bring to me. I'm okay with that, just worried about why he's moved in with her and what his…intentions, I guess, are. She's so naïve."

"Maybe not as much as you think she is. And Walter does need some help until his leg is better."

"That reminds me. You know the dead guy in the motel?"

Jackson put on a wary face. "What about him?"

"I know you can't tell me any details about his murder, but I wonder if he had anything to do with the wreck you told me about."

"You mean the one with the truck that was delivering your things from the plastic storage place?"

Tally sat back. "That truck had *our* plastics in it?"

"Yes, it was coming from the warehouse. The driver fell asleep at the wheel. He admitted it at the scene."

"But ours were delivered. Are you sure that wreck had *our* plastics on it? We got them and put them on display the very next day."

"The company sent out another truck that night, a smaller one, just for your order, since it was so close by. I think they put the rest of the cargo on another large truck and drove that the next day to wherever they were going. I think the shipment was ending up in Dallas."

"So, the man injured in the crash, the one who was sent to the hospital with a broken leg?"

Jackson got that wary look again. "What about him?"

"Is he the man who beat up Walter Wright? Someone beat Mr. Wright with a crutch when he tried to catch the crippled guy stealing the things from the window."

"We think so," he said slowly.

"I'm pretty sure I saw him. He was hanging around the next morning. We were all looking at the nice display. We were so happy with it until we noticed that the plastics were starting to melt in the sun coming through the glass window."

"And someone was there, with you, on crutches, at that time?"

"Yes. A whole crowd gathered and he was one of them. He seemed so interested in the window. He even ran into Lily and almost knocked her over. I think he was concentrating on the display and didn't look where he was going."

"That was probably him, then." Jackson nodded.

"And you haven't found him?"

"I didn't say that."

"I saw them take some DNA from the broken glass. Does it match the dead guy's?"

"It takes quite a while for the results to come back, but the 'dead guy,' as you call him, did have a cut on his hand."

"So, if he smashed the window and cut his hand, he probably has the rocks that were inside the plastic."

"No, actually. He didn't. And it's jade," Jackson said. "Very high quality jade."

"You had your uncle look at it?"

"Didn't have to. We had a jeweler here tell us. It's Burmese, he's certain."

Tally frowned. "So it actually is what we were talking about? It's Burmese and it comes from Myanmar?"

"Yes, people still call the jade Burmese Jade, mostly. I've heard it referred to as Myanmar Jade, too. It's the same thing." He grimaced and looked down. "It's also called Blood Jade."

"That sounds...awful. Like blood diamonds?"

"Yes, just like that. The people in that nation are being robbed of their jade, getting almost nothing out of it. The countryside is being ruined. People die when the mined mountains collapse on them. A lot of the mining is just plain illegal, besides being immoral."

"How did it end up here? In Fredericksburg? Inside our compostable plastic?"

"That is a very good question."

"Not legally, then."

"Most definitely not."

They ordered, ate a slow meal, and finished by sharing a dessert. The specter of the illegal gemstones receded and Tally had a wonderful evening. Jackson's work didn't even interrupt him, for once. There wasn't a single phone call or text for either one of them.

Later, at home with Nigel in her lap, though, she was again bothered by the Blood Jade Jackson had talked about. If it was mined illegally, was it being shipped the same way? Smuggled? Is that why it was hidden inside the candies? But how did it get there? Was that a mistake? Had a shipment meant for someone else gone to Yolanda? If the smugglers knew that Tally and Yolanda were involved, were they in danger?

Nigel gave her a direct look and blinked.

"You mean it might not be a mistake? It might have been meant to go to Bella's Baskets?"

He lifted a paw, licked it, and started grooming one ear.

"Don't be ridiculous. Yolanda wasn't receiving smuggled goods, Nige."

He paused, then started on the other ear.

"Jackson's not telling me everything. I know that. I sure wonder what he is holding back on. I don't see how any of this should be secret. If he does know where our thief is, he should announce that to the world. That's big news." Tally shook her head. "I don't understand what's going on at all."

9

Thursday morning, Raul was so quiet that Yolanda wondered if he was sick. She asked him twice if he was feeling okay and he said he was fine both times. The third time he snapped out the word. "Fine!" She knew she shouldn't ask him again, but clearly something was wrong.

They had several orders come in first thing in the morning, one for an older woman's birthday party—the giver of the gift basket wouldn't say how old the recipient was, but said she liked gardening and embroidery; another for the local garden club; and a third for a church luncheon, small baskets for centerpieces on over a dozen tables.

Her doctor had phoned in some new allergy pills for her when Yolanda told her they weren't working. These seemed much better. Her nose was completely clear. It was a good morning for Yolanda! She wished Raul felt as happy as she did.

Near lunchtime, a dark, handsome young man came in and hesitated just inside the door.

"Can I help y'all?" Yolanda called from farther back in the store.

"Is...is Raul here?" He ducked his head and looked around nervously.

"Oh, you must be his cousin, Mateo. Is that right?" Those Fuentes men were certainly good-looking, she thought. So was Kevin, her mind added, so as not to be disloyal to him.

Mateo nodded. "I need to see Raul."

"He just left to deliver a basket." The garden club basket had been easy and they had whipped that one out first. Mostly cut flowers arranged with three small potted plants and a lot of ribbon.

"Can I wait for him? I really need to talk to him."

"Sure. Have a seat." She pointed out the chairs that clients sometimes sat in to look at books with pictures of basket types and decoration ideas.

He sank into the chair and stared at the floor between his shoes. He seemed as despondent as Raul was today. Maybe she'd find out what was going on when the cousins talked to each other.

"Can I get you something to drink?" Yolanda asked. "Water or iced tea?" He shook his head without looking up at her.

Raul soon returned and stopped as soon as he was inside the door. He raised his eyebrows, surprised to see his cousin in the store. He was feeling something else, too, from the look in his narrowed eyes. Upset? Angry? His cousin jumped up as Raul stalked toward him.

"Teo! What are you doing here? Why would you come to my work?" Raul sounded annoyed. He halted in front of him and stood almost toe to toe with Mateo.

"Rulo, I need you to help me. I got fired again." Unlike Raul, Mateo had a soft, lilting accent. Yolanda thought she saw tears in Mateo's liquid brown eyes.

"What do you think I can do about that? I can't give you a job."

Mateo looked over at Yolanda with huge, shiny eyes.

"No, Mateo, I'm sorry," she said. "I can't afford to pay another employee."

Mateo slumped back into the chair, his shoulders sagging, his eyes going dull.

"Cuz, you can't keep losing jobs. Did you fall asleep delivering pizzas, too?"

Mateo glanced at Yolanda. "No. I didn't fall asleep. Why are you saying that?"

"Because you fell asleep at your last—"

"Rulo! *Cállate!*"

Yolanda's father was Italian, had been born there and come to America at a fairly young age and her mother was Latina, a Texan for generations. At home, when things got heated between them, they both lapsed into their first languages to argue. Spanish and Italian were enough alike that they could understand each other, and Yolanda picked up a lot of words in both languages. Especially, words that were rather unkind. She knew Mateo had just told his cousin to shut up.

"You've been in too many wrong places at the wrong times lately," said Raul. "I don't know what to think. You're mixed up in something bad."

Mateo threw one more look at Yolanda, a worried one, and hurried out the front door.

Raul stood, seething, looking daggers at his cousin's departing back. When Mateo disappeared, Raul shook his head and walked slowly to the table where Yolanda had the next basket half assembled. She had chosen a garden party theme for the older woman, since she was already doing the other garden-themed basket and planned on picking up a piece, or maybe several pieces, of embroidery for embellishment.

"Raul, what's going on? Why are you so mad at him? Why did he tell you to shut up?"

"He's...he's not hanging out with the right people."

"Is he the one you said was volunteering with the Crime Fritzers?"

Raul nodded as he picked up a colorful seed packet and tucked it into the basket beside a miniature sprinkling can.

"Are those the wrong people you're talking about?"

"No, no, not them." Raul shook his head. "But that wreck. The time he fell asleep. He was driving the truck that had our plastics in it."

"Are you saying you think he had something to do with the jade that was being smuggled?" She had talked about the jade with Raul after learning some of the details of it from Tally.

Raul looked at her with despair in his eyes. "I don't know what to think." He was almost wailing. "He's my cousin and I love him."

Yolanda shook her head. "We don't get to pick our relatives, do we?"

"But he's been acting so nervous lately. Like he's guilty of something."

"He got fired when he fell asleep, right?"

"Yes. And now he's gotten fired again, from his pizza delivery job, he says."

"Fired? Why was that? Do you know? It didn't have anything to do with smuggling, surely. You don't smuggle pizza."

Raul took a deep breath and looked at the ceiling. "I don't know. He delivered a pizza and the guy was dead."

"Oh! That was him? He found the guy in the motel?"

"He said he saw a wooden crutch on the floor before the police took him away to give them a statement."

Yolanda tried to put together the pieces of what Raul was telling her. She knew that the driver of the smaller truck had a broken leg from the accident that, apparently, Raul's cousin caused by falling asleep at the wheel, making a night delivery. Then the crime watch guy was beaten up with a crutch. And now a crutch showed up next to a dead guy that Mateo—the driver of the truck that broke the guy's leg—discovered.

"I don't know," she said. "This all sounds like bad luck to me. I don't see how any of this means that Mateo is mixed up with the smugglers."

Raul shrugged and arranged some plastic sprigs of greenery around the seed packets. "I just know something is wrong with him and he's acting strange. I've never seen him like this. He's nervous all the time. The way he's acting, it's just not like him." Raul's voice sounded flat, dejected.

"Have y'all asked him what's wrong?"

"He won't talk to me. Doesn't answer my questions, just changes the subject."

While Raul was gone making the last delivery of the day, Yolanda quietly called Kevin and asked if he could have dinner with her again.

"Sure. Name the time and place."

"This time I have something I'd like to talk to you about." If she discussed the situation with Mateo and Raul, maybe it would help her sort out what was going on, who was involved with what.

10

Yolanda was glad that her relationship with Kevin was on solid enough footing that he readily agreed to meet. They decided they would see each other for dinner in half an hour. She shooed Raul out early. It had been a good day for Bella's Baskets. Three new basket orders delivered and paid for. She hadn't taken a penny from her father in months. Maybe she was on her way to being self-sufficient and getting free from his controlling clutches. She knew her father loved her, but she needed to leave the stifling nest and fly. She couldn't consider herself a whole person unless—until, she corrected herself—*until* that happened.

She closed up the shop after Raul left and then called her little sister, Violetta.

"Yo, I was going to call you," she said, her voice bright. "I have some big news."

Yolanda heard what sounded like pure joy in Violetta's voice. "You sound like you're grinning."

"I am! Like a Cheshire cat or something. I'm crazy with smiling."

"Something to do with Eden?" Only the woman her sister loved could make her this happy, Yolanda thought.

"We're getting married! You're the first person I'm telling."

She'd been right. "Wonderful, Vi! Do y'all have a date?" Her sister deserved this after being shunned by her own parents for merely being who she was. Poor kid.

"Not yet. We're going to enjoy being engaged for a bit, then move to the next step. I never in my life thought this would happen to me."

Yolanda hesitated to bring up the subject of their parents. Mostly their father. "Are you going to…announce it?" She thought she was being oblique.

"You mean am I going to tell Papa?" Vi got it, oblique or not.

"Do you want me to?"

"I don't care if he never finds out, actually. He'll want nothing to do with it. With me. With us."

"That's not true, Vi. He loves you." At least he used to. Violetta had been their father's obvious favorite, up until the moment Vi announced that she had a girlfriend. He had switched his fierce devotion to Yolanda after that, to the daughter he had always ignored, but Yolanda felt nothing but resentment for the years he'd regarded her as the inferior, lesser daughter. Surely their papa still loved Violetta, deep inside. "Don't you think he'll come around when he hears you're getting married?"

"I do not."

"I'll let y'all know what he says. He might surprise us."

"You don't have to tell him. I don't intend to."

Yolanda congratulated her sister again and told her to give Eden a hug from her, but despondency descended as soon as the call ended and her false cheerfulness vanished. She knew Violetta was right. He would never forgive his daughter for being gay. Maybe he couldn't forgive himself for not knowing that about her, for not knowing who his daughter really was. But he would never succeed in making Yolanda into the substitute for the adored favorite he no longer had. She would not let that happen.

She shook off the feeling and got ready to see Kevin. It was her habit to keep a small bag handy at work that contained some large pieces of gold jewelry, extra makeup, a dressy pair of sandals with straps and heels, and a hairbrush and spray to fluff her wild mane into awesome dimensions. Just in case she got last-minute dinner invitations. Or, in this case, unless she delivered the invitation and it was, happily, accepted.

Kevin was already seated when she arrived, and was holding a table in the dimly-lit outdoor section of the restaurant, festooned with strands of dangling twinkle lights. Yolanda pulled out her chair, swishing her skirts and tossing her mane, accompanied by the ringing of the gold bangle bracelets that slid up and down her wrist as she sat.

"I got us some onion rings," he said. "And ordered a white for you."

With Kevin owning a wineshop and vineyard, he knew almost everything about wines. She knew he had ordered something good. He could be completely trusted on that subject. The glass sat at her place, keeping his glass company. He sometimes, not often, liked to go out to sample other local wines, so tonight they were in a restaurant associated with a rival wine merchant.

He raised his glass. "Here's to us." They clinked and he asked, "How's everything?"

"I think I'm just about recovered from the break-in. I lost money because we didn't do any business that day. But we had a very good day today. How about you?"

He grinned over the rim after his first sip. "I'm seeing my daughter next week."

"Kaycee?" Until two nights ago, she didn't know he had a daughter, let alone anything about her. Not even her name.

"She wants to connect with me. Now that her mother and I are apart, officially."

"How often do you see her?"

"Lately, not nearly enough. That will change, starting now."

He was obviously looking forward to seeing her. "How old is she?"

"A little younger than you. Rachel was very young when we got married."

Yolanda thought his daughter would have to be more than "a little" younger, but she was relieved that the daughter wasn't older. That would be... well, inappropriate. People would talk.

"That's nice," was all she could think of to say.

He seemed so happy about seeing his daughter that Yolanda would try very hard to be pleased for him. She hoped she could meet her soon, but didn't want to ask, for some reason.

The onion rings were delivered and Yolanda bit into the juicy part, enjoying being with Kevin, eating good food, with the knowledge her shop was doing well.

"Anything more about your broken window incident, and who was involved?" Kevin asked.

"Not really. Except for something Raul said today. That's what I wanted to talk to you about. His cousin came over. I think he wanted me to give him a job."

"A job at Bella's Baskets? That's strange. Isn't it?"

"He's a strange guy. He's been fired from two jobs very recently."

"He doesn't sound like a good risk. You're not hiring him, are you?"

Yolanda laughed. "I wouldn't hire him anyway. I can't afford to pay anyone else. But Raul was so upset."

"Why? Because he came to you?"

"No, for losing the jobs, I think. And he thinks something else is upsetting his cousin, but doesn't know what exactly."

"What kind of work does he do?"

Yolanda leaned closer and lowered her voice. "He was the driver of the truck for Planet Earth Plastics. The one that wrecked." She had looked up the invoice to be sure of the name of the manufacturer.

"So he's a truck driver. A bad one. Even more strange to want a job in a basket shop. Did he say anything about the wreck?"

"He fell asleep, he says."

"A very bad truck driver. What was the second job he lost?"

"Pizza delivery."

"Don't tell me. He wrecked a car for the pizza company?"

"I don't know, but I don't think so. He didn't say exactly why he was fired. But listen to this. Okay, first, he drove the truck that carried the smuggled jade. The truck driving job, obviously." She ticked off number one on her fingers. "Then, he delivered pizza to a guy who was dead when he got there." Yolanda ticked off the second finger.

"Bad luck for him. Poor guy." Kevin raised his wineglass for a sip, swirling his glass and observing the behavior of the liquid.

"He said that there were crutches in the room with the dead guy."

He set down his glass. "And the guy who broke your window was beaten up with crutches, wasn't he?"

"I think maybe the window-breaker was the one who beat up the dead man in the motel."

"It sounds like Raul's cousin is in that mess, deep. Up to his eyeballs."

"You think so? You yourself said it was bad luck."

"Nah, that's too much coincidence. Keep away from him. In fact, I wonder if Raul is involved, too."

"No!" Yolanda pointed her onion ring at Kevin. "He is not involved. Raul is a good kid."

Kevin gave her a skeptical look over the rim of his glass.

* * * *

When Tally got home, she noticed a message on her cell to call Detective Rogers. She kicked off her shoes, got a glass of iced tea, and sat on the couch. Which was a signal for Nigel to leap up next to her and lean on her arm, making it difficult to sip the tea and talk on the phone.

"You called?" she said when he answered. She could tell from the background noise that he was still at work. "Working late tonight?"

"I'm doing it for you." He chuckled. "Kind of, I guess. It's you and Yolanda that the victim robbed."

"Victim?"

"Yes, the guy in the motel, the one on crutches."

"Why are you calling him a victim? Was he the one found dead by the pizza guy?" She noticed a few new frayed places on her blue couch cushions. Was that Nigel's doing, or just old age on the part of the couch? Or both?

Jackson's voice got a lot more serious. "You didn't know that, did you? Maybe I shouldn't have let that spill. I figured you probably knew Mateo."

"Who's Mateo?" Tally struggled to juggle her tea, her phone, and her cat. Only a few drops of tea spilled onto her lap. She had heard that name. "Is he Raul's cousin?"

"You know what? I'm saying way too much. Ask Yolanda who he is. She should know."

As soon as Tally hung up, Yolanda called.

"Tally, can you talk right now?"

"Last time I checked." She started reciting the alphabet in a singsong voice.

"Smart aleck. Listen, I'm not sure what's going on, but maybe we can figure this out together."

"Figure what out?" Nigel bumped her arm with the top of his head. This time some tea fell on his dry, pristine fur. He bolted from the couch, highly insulted. Anyway, it was time for him to eat.

"Raul's cousin," Yolanda said.

"What about him?" Tally set her tea glass on the side table and went into the kitchen.

Tally heard Yolanda take in a deep breath before she plunged on. "Okay, Mateo showed up today asking me for a job and it turns out he was the driver for Planet Earth. *And* he was the person who found a dead guy with crutches in his room."

"Slow down, slow down. I'm assuming Raul's cousin is named Mateo, right?" Clutching her phone between her head and shoulder, she managed to get din-din into Nigel's bowl and set it on the floor.

"Right."

"Jackson told me the cousin found the guy on crutches." Tally sat on a kitchen stool and watched the chubby cat do his best to get chubbier.

"No, not *on* crutches. *With* crutches."

Tally was getting more confused by the minute. "Back up a minute. Raul's cousin is named Mateo."

"Correct."

"He asked you for a job, right? And he was driving for…Planet Earth?"

"He was the truck driver. The one who crashed the truck for Planet Earth, the plastic company Lily ordered our stuff from."

Yes, the company Lily had all the trouble with when the products melted in the sun. Lily had been calling them two or three times a day, trying to get their money back. It hadn't worked yet. "Oh. Poor guy."

"He probably got fired after that."

"Well, I'd say he's a poor guy then. He lost his job. So what about the crutches?"

"Raul said Mateo got a job after that delivering pizza. And he's the person who delivered the pizza to the guy with crutches in his room. Who was dead."

Tally had thought Jackson said the dead guy was the person who was on crutches, but maybe she misunderstood.

"What do you think, was the dead guy beaten to death by the same person who beat up the crime watch guy, the friend of your landlady?" Yolanda asked.

"Are you sure that's what happened? Maybe you confused some of it."

"Well, I did have some wine. Oh, I have to tell you the news! Vi and Eden are engaged. They're getting married!"

"Good for them," Tally said, glad to hear some good news for a change. "When and where? Are they registered?" Nigel had finished his food and had licked his whiskers. Now he sauntered out of the kitchen. Tally retrieved her glass and refilled it with ice cubes and decaf iced tea.

"I don't know the answers to any of that. Vi says they're going to enjoy being engaged for a while, then decide everything later."

"You know, that sounds smart. More people ought to do it that way." Then Tally sobered, remembering the family situation. "Oh, what do your parents say?"

"Nothing, since they don't know yet."

"When is Vi telling them?"

"She isn't. I can't decide if I should or not. They're all basically not speaking to each other."

"So your sister could conceivably get married and your parents might never even know?"

"You're right," Yolanda said, sounding like she'd just made up her mind. "They have to at least know about it. They don't have to go, or to give them a gift, or even give them their blessing, but they have to know."

Tally sipped her tea after the call ended, worried about the Bella family, along with everything else. Nigel crouched at her feet, wary of the wetness in her glass and Tally rubbed his side with her toes. That seemed to be satisfactory to both of them.

* * * *

Thet Thura studied the young man sitting beside him in the front seat. Arlen was in the back, his long legs tucked up under his chin, sitting beside the older man. The truck smelled like beer, cigarettes, and something else unpleasant that was probably some local marijuana. It smelled like the weed the people in Dallas smoked. The young man said his name was Ira Mann. Americans had such odd names. Mateo had introduced them after much urging from Thet. Mateo had mentioned that Ira and a few others in the crime watch group were stealing valuable things. Maybe getting to know some local thieves would be a way to find out where the last few missing pieces of jade were. Maybe one of them had even swiped the precious gems. His Uncle Win wouldn't rest until it was all accounted for.

"We look for a house with the lights out and no cars around," Ira was telling him, as they sat in Ira's dirty white pickup truck. Thet thought it was smart of him to drive such a vehicle. It seemed that most people in Texas drove white pickup trucks, so he wouldn't ever be obvious. "Then we go in the back. A lot of times the back doors are unlocked, even if the front door isn't."

They were cruising slowly down the street.

"Ira," said the other man in the back seat. "We have to hit a different street. We've done Schubert too many times."

"Yeah, you're right, Kyle," Ira answered, and made a few turns to get onto another street that looked just like the last one.

"What kinds of things do you find?" Thet asked. "Jewels? Gemstones?"

"Sometimes," Ira said. "Small electronics are good. You'll see."

"There," Kyle in the back seat said, "that house on the corner. Go around to the next street."

"We don't ever park in front of the house," Ira said, like he was giving instructions. "There aren't any alleys here, so we have to leave the truck down a few houses."

Thet did wonder if the two men thought they were training him and Arlen to do this job. They didn't know Arlen's name, let alone that he lived in Dallas. Thet just wanted to pick their brains. He and Arlen weren't going to stick around this town after he found his missing property.

"Okay, come on," Ira said, climbing out of the truck.

"We can stay here," Thet said.

The other two men exchanged a look.

"No, you don't," Kyle said. "You come with us."

"I'll come, but Arlen can be lookout," Thet said.

That seemed to be okay with them.

Did they think he would steal the truck? Thet got out and walked behind them, back to the house on the corner. He was surprised they didn't change clothes, or wear dark masks, or somehow disguise themselves. On American television shows, thieves always did that. They also carried weapons, or tools for breaking and entering. The only things these two were carrying were plastic bags they had stuffed into the back pockets of their jeans. Thet assumed those were to carry out their loot.

It was about two o'clock in the morning. Everyone in Fredericksburg except them seemed to be asleep. The only noises were insects in the trees, and a strident, regular, squealing sound. "What is that?" he asked.

Kyle cocked his head. "Oh, them's just tree frogs. You don't have those where you're from?"

"We do have the tree frogs. But their call is different." Thet tried to mimic their delicate peeping, but they chuckled at him and he quit. How dare they laugh at him.

They opened the wooden gate into the backyard of the house they were targeting. It gave a loud screech and all three men froze, cringing. Nothing happened, so they made their way quietly to the back door.

Thet thought that having three men along was cumbersome and gave them a better chance of getting caught. He decided to stay outside and told them that.

"Sure," Ira said. "You can be our backyard lookout. If anyone comes, do that frog sound."

Thet thought that the sound of an Asian frog might not blend in with the night noises here, but didn't argue. He had no intention of warning them of anything. If someone approached, he would disappear.

When they found that the back door was securely locked, it was a letdown for all of them, even Thet. He was surprised by his disappointment, since he didn't want to be there in the first place. Now is when lock-picking equipment would have come in handy. Stupid American thieves. How did they ever steal anything?

"Just drop us back at the motel," he said, not bothering to conceal his disgust.

From now on, he would concentrate on Walter Wright, or maybe Mateo. Either one of them was probably a better way to find out where the missing jade was.

11

Halfway through the day on Friday, as Tally was finishing up a sale for a customer, she cocked her head to listen more closely to the woman Dorella was helping.

The woman's voice was strident and carried well, filling up the salesroom. "You have to tell me where you got that ring! You have to." She grabbed Dorella's hand, inspecting the pinkie ring Ira Mann had given her.

At first Tally thought she was excited because she liked Dorella's pretty new ring. Dorella drew back an inch or two at the intensity and volume from the woman, who was middle-aged, well-dressed in slacks and a silk blouse, probably on her lunch hour from work.

"It was a gift," Dorella said, snatching her hand back and curling her fingers protectively.

"Who gave it to you?" the woman demanded, a fierce frown marring her smooth face.

Tally realized it wasn't excitement in her manner. She was acting belligerent. Tally completed her sale and, as that customer went out the door, came over to Dorella and the woman confronting her. "Is there something I can help you with?" she asked the customer.

"I want to know where she got that ring." The woman was almost spitting, becoming more and more hostile.

"Why?" Tally asked. "I don't think that concerns you." She caught Dorella's eye and tipped her head toward the kitchen. Dorella fled through the door.

"Wait!" the woman called, starting to go after her. "That's my ring!"

Tally stepped in front of her so she couldn't pursue Dorella. "Please tell me what you're talking about. I can't have you acting this way to my employees."

"Just the one. That one employee. She stole my ring."

Was this woman crazy? She had to quiet her down and get her out of here. "I'm sure she didn't. Please leave my store. Right now."

"You'll be hearing from me." The woman stalked out, slamming the front door and jangling the chimes. Tally's mouth dropped open.

Lily burst through the kitchen door. "What happened? Dorella's crying and won't tell me what's going on."

Tally wasn't sure, herself, what was going on. "A customer thinks that Dorella's ring was stolen from her."

"Dorella would never steal her ring. Who was she?"

"I have no idea."

Lily and Dorella were getting along well, now that Lily had apologized for being so rude the first day Dorella wore her ring. And now this happened. That ring was not bringing good things for poor Dorella.

Tally found out who the woman was just before closing. She and Lily and Dorella were in the kitchen, cleaning up the last of the evidence of a spate of afternoon cooking, and Molly was in front, polishing the glass case, emptied for the night, when the office phone rang. Tally ran to get it.

"Tally, I know it's time for you to close, but I need you to stay there for a few more minutes." It was Detective Jackson Rogers.

"What's up?" She would be happy to have dinner with him, but why was he asking her to stay at the shop?

"I'll tell you when I get there. Is Dorella Diggs there? Make sure she stays, too."

Tally's heart sank. She had a feeling the accusatory customer was going to make trouble for them. He wouldn't tell her more. She would have to wait and see what she could find out.

She hung up and asked Dorella, "Do you know where Ira got your new ring?"

"Was that the woman who is accusing me of stealing it? No one stole her ring. Like there aren't two identical rings in the world."

"You need to stick around. Detective Rogers needs to talk to you for a minute. He's on his way. I'm sure we can clear everything up."

"Don't worry," Lily said. "Ira can probably just show them a receipt or something. That woman is awful. Can we bar her from the store, Tally?"

Tally shook her head. "What would happen if we did that? You saw what she's like."

"She'd probably bring in the cops and a reporter." Dorella laughed as she said it.

However, she was grim by the time Jackson got there. Tally thought she was frightened.

She went to slip the *closed* sign on the door and jumped when a horn sounded outside. Tally realized she was holding her whole body tight, she was so full of tension. She rolled her neck to loosen it and looked out the front window. A pickup truck with a sign on the door that said *Howie's Garage* was at the curb.

Molly whisked by, a huge smile on her face. "Bye, Ms. Holt," she called over her shoulder. Tally felt the breeze as she tugged the door open and ran out. Molly and Howie. That, at least, was good.

After the detective talked with Dorella, which didn't seem to get him anywhere, he told Tally he was leaving to talk to Ira Mann. "The woman who wants to file charges was very convincing. She had a break-in recently. She also had a jeweler's receipt for a ring identical to Dorella's, and had even taken pictures of it."

"Do you think Ira could have stolen it?" Tally asked. All of her employees had all left by then and she and Jackson were now chatting in the kitchen over cups of coffee. The lights in the shop were turned out, except the security lights in the front and a dim one she always left on over the sink. The shadows cast on his face in the faint lighting made his rugged face look even stronger than it usually did. His gray eyes glinted, looking almost black. He didn't answer.

Tally shook her head. "He couldn't be a thief. They're trying to catch the thieves. He's part of the crime watcher group, Jackson. They're putting on extra patrols, he said, because there have been some residential break-ins. A lot of them. Is that true?"

Jackson rubbed his chin with a gritty sound. This late in the day, his beard was becoming visible on his usually clean-shaven face. "There are some things going on."

"And you can't tell me about them, right?" Tally snapped. Why couldn't he ever tell her anything? "Ira is the son of the new fire chief. You don't think he's breaking into houses, do you?"

"As I said, there are things going on. And no, you're right, I can't tell you about them. At least not right now."

He left and Tally assumed he was headed for the Manns' place to talk to Ira. For the briefest of moments, she wondered if Dorella would have warned Ira, and if she knew he'd stolen the jewelry, or if she had helped steal it. She shook her head. She was not going to think thoughts like that.

Talking of the Crime Fritzers made her wonder how Mrs. Gerg was doing with her houseguest. Every time she thought about it, Walter Wright moving in like that alarmed Tally. She would dash home, feed Nigel, and then check on Mrs. Gerg. Maybe she could subtly ask Walter about the mystery men, the one he called Thet and the other one, the cowboy.

After she took care of darling Nigel, Tally headed out on her mission on foot. As she neared Mrs. Gerg's house, she looked up as someone crossed to the other side of the street. She couldn't make out who it was, but the person seemed to have come from Mrs. Gerg's. It certainly wasn't Walter. He was still using a crutch and limping. The figure was too tall to be the mysterious dark-skinned man, Thet Thura. His height matched the cowboy, but there was no big ten-gallon hat. As the person passed in front of a house with a gas lamp, she saw long blond hair shining in the light. The gait wasn't feminine, though. Was it Ira? She would have waved if he had looked up as he passed her on the other side, but he kept his head down. Maybe he was patrolling this block. And alone, just like he was not supposed to be doing. If he was even a member of the crime patrol. He hadn't been at the meeting in the home of Olive Baum. The man she talked to didn't even say he was his partner.

Walking up Mrs. Gerg's front sidewalk, Tally could hear Walter's raised voice through the door. She couldn't distinguish his words, but he didn't sound happy. Once again, she felt the back of her neck prickle. Wanting to interrupt whatever was going on and concerned for Mrs. Gerg, Tally rapped on the door.

"Well, answer it!"

Tally understood his words this time.

Mrs. Gerg opened the door an inch or two, her worried eyes peering out through the crack, her shoulders hunched—fearing who might be there? Tally wondered. When she saw Tally she broke into a huge smile and flung the door open.

"Come in, come in. Come have a seat."

Walter sat on the couch, scowling, as Tally walked into the living room, full of heavy furniture, most of it adorned with doilies. Before she sat, she asked Mrs. Gerg if she needed anything, remembering that she'd brought groceries over last time she came here when Mrs. Gerg told her she couldn't leave Walter.

"No, nothing right now."

"Be sure and tell me if I can run any errands for you," Tally said. "Are you getting out to shop now? Are you doing better, Mr. Wright?" She perched on a black-and-white plaid upholstered chair.

"Better how?" He almost snarled.

Tally looked at Mrs. Gerg, who kept her eyes on Walter Wright. Tally couldn't read her expression. Was she afraid of him?

"How's everything going here?" she asked.

"Come over here," Walter said, looking at Mrs. Gerg and softening his voice and demeanor.

She grinned and plopped down next to him.

"That's my girl." He put his good arm around her and rubbed her shoulder. "We're doing just fine," he said to Tally. "Candy takes such good care of me."

"Are you getting out to yard sales?" Tally asked Mrs. Gerg. "I saw an ad for a big one starting tomorrow."

When the older woman shook her head with a sad look, Tally said, "I hope you can soon. I know how much you love that." She threw a pointed glance at Walter Wright when she said that last part. "How soon can you move back home?" she asked him.

Mrs. Gerg gave him an anxious look. Was her anxiety because she wanted him to leave, or was she afraid of him leaving? It was hard to tell.

The man raised his leg a couple of inches and pointed to the surgical boot on his foot. "I still have a broken arm and leg. I guess you can see that."

"Yes, that must be very hard." Tally tried to put syrupy sympathy into her voice. "Have your friends been back?"

"Friends?" Walter scowled again.

"Yes, the men who came to call on you when I was here before. What were their names?"

Mrs. Gerg answered, "Thet was one of them. Isn't that such an unusual name? He's from another country. He and the other man brought some business things over just the other day."

Tally saw Mrs. Gerg flinch. Had Walter pinched her?

Tally spoke to Walter again. "What country is Thet from? How do you know him?"

"He's here on business. Candy, could you get me some pain pills? Right now?" He turned to Tally. "I need to get some rest."

She could take a hint. If she stayed and Mrs. Gerg answered any more of her questions, she was afraid he'd keep pinching her. As soon as Candy returned with some pills and a glass of water, Tally fled the strained atmosphere, determined to check in on Mrs. Gerg every day for a while.

As she drove away, she passed a white van with a blue sign on the side, going in the direction of Mrs. Gerg's house. She didn't get a good look and couldn't read the whole sign, but the last word was *Shop*. Her neck prickled once more.

12

When Tally got home she called Yolanda. She was about to explode from everything around her being messed up and unresolved. What she wanted was a quiet, orderly life, making and selling candies and sweet treats. Her early childhood, spent with her traveling musician parents, had given her enough upheaval and chaos for a lifetime. She had never liked living like that, though her parents loved it. When Yolanda had talked her into coming back to Fredericksburg, buying the building next to hers, and settling down, she had known it was the right thing to do. It was what she'd been longing for her whole life, but hadn't realized it until Yolanda's insistence that she move back to Fredericksburg. She'd been lacking a stable location, people who stayed put. And much less hullabaloo, like she had had with her parents. She had now achieved all but that last one.

The thought that she was being disloyal to her loving parents flitted through her mind. The fact was, they thrived on the life they led, while Tally would have wilted and shriveled leading a nomadic existence like that for her whole adult life. Her brother Cole seemed to live a life in between those two extremes. He traveled for his work, doing his artistic sculpture installations, but had a home base where he did his preinstallation work, a place he could go to, a place he could park his Volvo and call home. True, it was in Oklahoma and he wasn't there very much, but their parents didn't have a single place they could return to, except maybe, now, Tally's place.

"Tally? What's going on?"

Tally breathed a sign of relief hearing her friend's voice. "I need to talk to someone sane."

Yolanda laughed. "And you picked me? You're hard up, aren't you?"

"Everything's a mess. Where are you? I need to see you."

Yolanda was at home in her Sunday House. The place had an interesting origin. Hers was one of several small remaining historic houses that had been built in Fredericksburg in the late 1800s by local German ranchers as second homes. Sometimes called *Sonday house* in the peculiar local German-ish dialect, they had been used by the original families on weekends when they came to town for church. Yolanda's was typical in construction, two rooms downstairs and a third on the top half-story, which had sloping ceilings. Hers had an outdoor staircase to the upper floor that she used for storage. Of the Sunday Houses that still survived, some were tourist attractions, some were rented, and a few were lived in by their owners. These last, the ones now being living in, had usually been renovated to include built-on kitchens and bathrooms. All were pricey. Yolanda could only afford to live where she did because of her wealthy parents. Though Tally knew that it galled her to be so dependent on them, she also knew that Yolanda loved her beautiful, unique home.

Tally stepped onto the small porch and rapped on Yolanda's door.

* * * *

When Yolanda heard Tally's knock, she threw the door open. Tally looked distraught, so Yolanda set about fetching wineglasses from the kitchen and a bottle of Kevin's best red wine. As she worked the corkscrew, Tally perched on the edge of the brocade couch.

They clinked glasses and each had a sip. "Okay. Spill," Yolanda said. "I have some burning issues I have to talk to you about, too."

"Where to start?" Tally looked at the ceiling while Yolanda took a seat in her wingback chair.

"What's burning the hottest in your mind?" Yolanda asked.

"The most recent problem, I guess. Mrs. Gerg. I'm worried about her."

Yolanda listened to her tell about the tension she'd perceived between Mrs. Gerg and Walter Wright.

"Mentally abusive?" Yolanda asked.

"Maybe. She's at least dangerously besotted."

Yolanda considered that for a moment. "Dangerous? Just because she's older doesn't mean she can't get besotted. It can be good for a person."

"You're right. She has the right to be happy. It's just that I don't know anything about him. I'm not sure he's treating her well. He might be taking advantage of her. I thought he was yelling at her before I knocked."

"She's a big girl, Tally."

"He doesn't seem to have any family who can take care of him. She's doing it all."

"Does he have any friends?"

Tally took a moment to think about that. "Well, there were the two guys who came to the door while I was there. That's the only time I've seen Walter leave her couch."

"What guys?"

"One of them had an odd name. Thet, Walter said. Maybe Thet Thorough? Something like that. The other one was a tall cowboy type with a chaw."

"Who are they? Are they from around here?"

"Never saw them before. Thet is a short, darker-skinned Asian man. The tall guy didn't say a word, but he seems American. I think they were asking about the crime watch thing. I don't know why, but he gives me the creeps. Just now I tried to find out something more about them and Mrs. Gerg said Thet is from another country. When I asked which one, Walter cut her off. She said they brought over 'some business things' and I could swear Walter pinched her when she said that. She jumped! Then he told her to get him some pain pills and told me he had to take a nap. So I left. He's taking up her whole life."

Yolanda took another sip of her wine, frowning. "You said that was a good thing. It keeps Mrs. Gerg from scrounging up yard-sale junk to give to yours truly."

Tally winced. "I didn't put it like that."

"No, but that's what you meant. Pinching her isn't good, though. What are you going to do?"

"I'm going to keep going over there to check up on her. I get the impression those other two guys are doing something shady with Walter. I wonder if they're the people stealing things and since they're on the crime watch, it would make it easier. It seems like Walter doesn't want me to know anything about them and their dealings. That reminds me… there's something else about that crime watch. You know Dorella is dating the fire chief's son, Ira Mann, right?"

Yolanda nodded. Dorella seemed almost as fickle as Tally's brother. She thought Dorella and her brother Cole had made a good pair, but they weren't together anymore. While they were, Yolanda had gotten over her longtime resentment of Cole for his past shabby treatment of her, at least. Yolanda had been one in a long line of his love-em-and-leave-em women.

"A couple of things," Tally continued. "I think I might have seen Ira on Mrs. Gerg's block tonight. But maybe he was patrolling or something. If he *is* a member of the patrol."

"The other thing?"

"A customer was in my shop today and practically attacked Dorella."

"Attacked her? What for? Was she hurt?"

"Not physically. Just...she thought Dorella had stolen her ring, the one Ira gave to her. The woman even went to the police and reported that Dorella has her jewelry."

"So..." Yolanda put two and two together in her mind. "Do you think Ira stole it?"

Tally shrugged. "I'm not sure. I've been trying to decide. Why would he? If he's on the team that's trying to prevent the stealing that's been going on. Tell me again what you heard about the crutches and the dead guy."

"Raul says Mateo saw crutches in the room when he tried to deliver the pizza."

"How did he see into the room? If the guy was dead, he wouldn't answer the door, would he?"

Yolanda's mind spun. "You're right. Maybe he said the door was open. Or unlocked."

"If that guy was beaten to death with crutches, that makes two attacks. Him and Walter Wright. Walter was trying to stop a thief. What was this guy doing?"

"Walter's probably lucky to be alive, then."

"I don't get it, though," Tally said. "I don't think it would be easy to kill someone with a crutch. Walter was beat up enough to go to the hospital, but he's not really that bad. He didn't stay long. A broken arm and a messed-up foot."

"Was the bad guy interrupted when he was with Walter, attacking him? Inside the motel room there would be more time and privacy."

"Maybe? All I know is that someone still has the jade that was smuggled and stolen from your window."

"Maybe this motel guy was beaten because he was part of the smuggling ring and someone was trying to get him to talk? Speaking of stealing, I need to talk to you about Raul and his cousin, Mateo."

"So Mateo found the dead guy and saw into the Motel Eleven room..." Tally thought out loud, not registering what Yolanda had just said. "Then he opened the door somehow. It was unlocked? But why would the murderer leave without locking the door? It seems unlikely."

"Tally! Let me talk!" Yolanda interrupted, her face full of concern but also a sense of affection for her friend and her busy mind. "Raul is very worried about Mateo, but I can't get Raul to say exactly why. I know that he's lost a couple of jobs lately, but it seems like more than that. Something...criminal."

"Does... Raul think he killed the guy in the motel room?"

Yolanda shook her head, sending her big gold hoop earrings swinging. "I don't know. He won't say, but I can't help but wonder."

"You don't suppose—no, that couldn't be right. But, with that door thing. That's pretty strange."

"What? Tell me what you were going to say, Tally." Yolanda was afraid Tally was going to voice the same dark thought she'd been having.

"Well, Raul. His cousin was driving the truck that carried the smuggled jade. There has to have been more than one person in on that scheme."

"No." Just no. Raul wasn't doing anything illegal.

"You said Raul is worried. Maybe not about his cousin. Maybe about both of them. Do you think they were together in this?"

There, Tally had said what Yolanda hadn't been letting herself think.

* * * *

As soon as Tally got inside her house, her mother called.

"Where are you?" Tally asked. "Still in Gibraltar?" She glanced at the time, a little past eleven. She was so tired. In Gibraltar, it would be around five in the afternoon, being six hours ahead. She tried to keep track of her parents by noting what time it was wherever they were. It helped her to be able to picture them in their surroundings during their phone calls.

"Not very much longer. We have tickets to fly out, but there's some sort of problem. I'm not sure what it is. The whole airport is buzzing. No one seems to be going anywhere. We've been here since early this morning trying to rebook our flight."

"Is it something political?" Tally knew nothing of the politics of Gibraltar, but wondered what else would disrupt a whole airport.

"No, no, nothing like that. Something with the bookings. Your father is talking to some people at the counter right now. I'm sure he'll figure it out."

"How did your shows go? Did they like you there?" Considering the many different countries they traveled to and the many different cultures they performed before, she always wondered how their act translated. Her parents never seemed to have any problems in that area. She wandered into her bedroom, ready to collapse.

"We're very happy about how it went. The place held four-hundred-fifty people and we filled it all but two nights. It was almost full those nights, too. And there aren't that many people here. It's a small place. Anyway, we're ready to get to the next engagement."

"Where are you going next?" Her mother sometimes texted their itinerary, but it was so detailed—they went so many places, most of them places Tally had never been, some of them places she had never heard of—so she had trouble keeping their schedule straight in her mind.

"We're booked in Rome."

"That sounds great. Good Italian food, right?"

"Not only that, you'll never guess where we're playing. The Circus Maximus!"

"There's a theater near there?"

"No, no. We'll be on a stage *in* the Circus Maximus. Right there inside it." Her mother sounded more excited than usual about the next venue. Tally could hardly blame her. She couldn't imagine performing in an ancient Roman site like that.

"They let you do that?"

"Oh yes. They have rock concerts there. All sorts of things. Wait a sec." Her mother paused to listen to the speaker that Tally could also hear. "They just called our flight. We're boarding now. Love you."

Tally looked up the news from Gibraltar on her phone after she hung up. She didn't find anything specific to that one place, but it looked like there were problems with European travel all over the continent. A big vacation booking agency had gone bankrupt without any warning and stranded thousands of travelers throughout Europe and even beyond. The problems affected travelers in the US, the Caribbean, and other places. Should she be worried about her parents? If anyone knew how to get around, it was Bob and Nancy Holt, who lived on their performing circuit, wherever that may be for the day.

It was time for her to call her brother, Cole.

He surprised her by answering right away.

"Hey, Sis. Everything okay in Eff Burg?"

"Not really, but they're worse in Gibraltar."

"Huh? Oh, are Mom and Dad in Gibraltar? What's going on there?"

"They've been stranded at the airport because a big tour company has gone bankrupt and flights are disrupted all over Europe. But Mom said they were calling their flight to Rome just before she hung up."

"Do you think they'll be okay?"

Tally had no idea. "I think so, but I'm not positive." She needed to find out more about this tour company problem.

"Speaking of Eff Burg—"

"That was you, not me," she said. "You spoke of it."

"Yeah, I'm speaking of it." He laughed. "How's Dorella? She doing all right?"

How much should she tell him? Tally threw her head back and looked to the ceiling for the answer. "Um, she, um…"

"What? What's wrong with her?"

"Did you know she's been seeing the new fire chief's son, Ira Mann?"

"She told me that."

"You've talked to her?"

"We call. Text sometimes. Just to keep in touch."

"She didn't tell you about… well, Ira gave her a ring…"

"They're engaged? She did not tell me that."

Tally couldn't tell from his tone if he was jealous or not. Probably not, since he had never yet gone back to a woman he dumped. "I don't think it's an engagement ring. Just a pretty ring. She's wearing it on her pinkie. The thing is, one of my customers said it's hers. That it's been stolen."

"Little Ira is a thief?"

Tally didn't think he was all that little—in fact, he was built big, like his dad. But she did think he might be a thief.

"I'll have to get in touch with her," he said. "See what's going on. Hey, Sis, don't worry about Mom and Dad. You know they always land on their feet."

They usually did. Except sometimes when they didn't. At least she had shared the burden with her brother. It felt lighter. She plopped onto her bed, relieved their parents were getting on a plane on the way to their next destination, and hoping they would be fine.

13

Yolanda was pleased to see Raul already at work when she got there Saturday morning. She started to sing out a "hi" when she noticed some water spilled on the floor and went to the sink in the back to get something to sop it up. She heard Raul's voice around the corner, in the supply closet, and stopped to listen, wondering who he'd be talking to.

"No, that's not what I'm saying. I didn't ask for a raise…Because I know I can't get one…Everybody always needs more money, Teo. Just because I could use it doesn't mean—Teo, you're gonna have to get another job…"

Yolanda held her breath. She didn't want Raul to think she was eavesdropping on him. He must think he should get a raise. But he hadn't asked for one. Surely he knew she couldn't afford it yet. Maybe that's what he meant.

"Don't worry about that. You didn't kill Sutton, so they can't get you for that…I know you worked together. That doesn't mean you killed him…They don't know you were doing that. Nobody knows who's doing the smuggling, do they? Just keep quiet and no one will find out…You had *better* keep quiet. You know those people. They'll kill you. The rest? What do you mean, the rest? There's more?" A brief silence, then Raul said goodbye.

Yolanda stood still and silent, shocked at what she was hearing. Raul and Mateo. And smuggling. She grabbed the roll of paper towels sitting on the counter and glided soundlessly to the front. She knelt and began mopping up the puddle before she called out.

"Raul? Are you here? Did you spill something?"

"I'm back here." Raul appeared around the corner. "Oh no. I must have tipped the vase when I took out the flowers." He held a bunch of lilies and a basket, his phone nowhere to be seen.

Yolanda started sneezing as soon as the lilies were within five feet, even though she'd taken her new allergy pill that morning. So much for that. She would try to remember to always stay away from lilies in the spring when her defenses were being pounded by everything blooming outside. Maybe she would quit using lilies. There were lots of other flowers.

She waited the rest of the day for Raul to ask her for a raise, if his cousin had talked him into it. But he never did.

* * * *

It had been a long, busy day. Tally was so tired she could hardly stand up, but Yolanda sounded like she needed to talk. "I'll meet you for a glass of iced tea, okay? Then I have to get home. We had an incredible day." It seemed that the more complicated her life got, the busier her store became.

Yolanda agreed to a brief meeting. "It won't take long, but I just have to tell you something. Just so you know."

Tally bent to put the last of the baking sheets away in the cupboard.

"I'm off, Tally," Lily called from the front. She usually stayed until every single thing was in order. But she had other things on her mind lately, Tally knew.

"Have fun tonight," she called to Lily.

Lily ran back to the kitchen. "Am I that obvious? How do you know we're going out tonight?"

Her young love warmed Tally's heart. "Just have a good time. Say hi to Raul."

Lily gave her a sheepish look.

"I'm glad you're feeling good today. How are things with you and your cousin Amy?"

Lily frowned. "Not all that good. I've tried to sit down and talk things out with her, but she won't do it."

"What do you mean? She won't talk to you?"

"Every time I mention working things out, she gets cold as ice and says she has to leave, has to call someone, has to go in her bedroom and do something. She might as well say she has to wash her hair."

"That's tough."

"We've always gotten along okay, but we were never bosom buddies or anything. We probably shouldn't live together. I can't afford a place on my own, though." She gave a slight smile.

"But?" Tally asked, at that smile.

"Something might work out. You just never know."

After she left, Tally wondered if she was thinking of moving in with Raul. Sure sounded like it. She hoped Lily didn't make a hasty move before she was ready for it.

Tally finished tidying, gathered her things, and was locking up. Before she got out the door, though, Detective Jackson Rogers called her.

"Have you seen this morning's paper?" he asked.

She hadn't, but her copy from home, still folded, was on her desk, unread. "What do you want me to see?" She headed back into the office to get it. She picked it up and shook it open.

"Look at the first page and tell me if you've ever seen the man who's pictured."

She opened it up and saw that the name and picture of the Motel 11 victim were displayed on the front page. With a start of recognition, she answered him. "Yes, that's the guy!"

"What guy, Tally? Tell me exactly."

"He's the one on crutches. The one who was looking at our window when the plastic was first melting. He's the one who bumped into Lily and almost knocked her down."

The name Sawyer Sutton was under his picture and the article began by asking if anyone had any information on the "mystery" victim.

"He's the one that's dead? Who is he?" she asked.

"We can't find much information on him. That's why we're making the public plea. Do you know anything else about him?"

The dead guy was *on* crutches. Was he also killed with them? "How did he die?"

"I'm not at liberty to say yet."

"I mean, was he beat up with the crutches, like Walter Wright was?"

"He might be the person who attacked Mr. Wright. But we don't know what their connection is. But Sawyer was strangl—he wasn't beaten with crutches."

"I thought," Tally said, "that Walter Wright got beat up trying to get back our plastic."

"Pretty severe consequence for that, don't you think? A fight over pieces of plastic?"

"You think it's all about the jade stones. The ones that were inside the plastic. Do you think they all knew about them? This Sutton guy and Walter Wright? Were they fighting over them?" Or had Walter just been trying to catch a thief in the act? As a good Crime Fritzer?

"I shouldn't say anything more. But if you know anyone who knows this guy, or anything about him, let me know."

She promised she would as she stuck the newspaper into her purse and darted out the door to meet Yolanda. She was the one who said they should have a quick, short meeting. As she walked to the small café, she realized Jackson was right. Walter probably didn't get beat up because he was trying to retrieve cheap, melting pieces of plastic, to save them from being stolen. Why hadn't she thought of that before? Had *he* known there was valuable jade inside of them? Or had he seen the jade as Sawyer Sutton was stealing it? How much jade had actually been there? Enough to kill someone over? Jackson hadn't been sure that there was more, other than just that the few pieces she found of the valuable Burmese jade.

Yolanda was waiting with two glasses of wine already poured, at a table in the corner, when Tally walked into the small, dim dining room. Hadn't she suggested iced tea? Tally wasn't used to drinking wine every single night. She would have to take a wine vacation soon.

This wasn't a place that tourists visited and it wasn't crowded, even though this was Saturday night. Before Tally could get completely seated, Yolanda started in.

"I'm so worried about Raul," she said. "I walked in on him talking to Mateo this morning. He didn't know I was there."

"Hi, I'm doing fine today. Did you have a good one?" Tally countered, raising her glass and taking a sip. "Thanks for fortifying me. What am I in for?" This obviously wasn't the time to give up the wine for a while.

"Sorry. Yes, we had a good day. Well, not me. I've been worried sick all day. And my darn allergies." She wiped a sniffle with a tissue from her purse.

"Why, pray tell? What was Raul saying?"

"He was talking about Mateo working with someone named Sutton, who had been killed, of all things, and he sounded like he was talking about them doing illegal things."

"Them? Sutton and Mateo? Look at this." She fished the paper out of her purse and held up the picture labeled *Sawyer Sutton*. "He's the guy Raul's cousin found dead."

Yolanda squinted at the paper in the dim light, took it and got a closer look. "Wait, he's the one who was on the sidewalk with us."

"Yes, the one who ran into Lily."

"He's dead? And Mateo found him dead? And…Mateo worked with him, Raul said. I think."

"So they were both smuggling that jade?" Tally filled Yolanda in on Jackson's evaluation of the green stones and their value. "If all our plastic had the stones inside, there was a lot of jade in your window. Worth a lot of money. Are people fighting over it? Getting killed because of it?

"You know," Tally continued, "Jackson said they don't know much about the guy, Sawyer Sutton. Maybe Raul could tell them who he is and where he's from."

"Maybe. I'll ask Raul to talk to the police about that, if he can. I'm glad no one knows about the other pieces of plastic. The ones we haven't used yet."

"Oh my gosh! There *are* more, aren't there?" She'd forgotten about the extra pieces they hadn't used. "We need to show them to the police."

"I'll get them and bring them to the station first thing in the morning," Yolanda said. "They're in one of my cupboards."

"Does Raul know they're there?" Would he steal them and help his cousin get them to their smuggling destination? "Are you sure they're still there?"

"I—I don't know. I haven't looked."

"Lily and Raul are seeing a lot of each other right now. Poor Lily. I hope Raul isn't involved with anything illegal. She's already upset enough about the plastic melting, and everything else related to it." What if Lily was thinking about moving in with Raul? That was a good possibility. Should she tell Lily about the suspicions swirling around her beau?

Tally prayed the pieces were still where Yolanda had left them. If they weren't, that probably meant Raul had stolen them. She didn't tell Yolanda that Lily and Raul were out together right now, at this moment. It was at least the second time they'd gone out, but there were probably more times she didn't know about.

There was one thing for sure. She didn't want Lily's heart broken.

* * * *

Yolanda decided she couldn't wait for morning. She had to know if the extra, unused candy pieces were still there, in her cupboard where she'd left them. She didn't suspect Raul, she told herself. Not really. She just had to...reassure herself.

After Tally left for home, she returned to Bella's Baskets, going in the back way, through the alley. She didn't quite want to admit why she was being secretive and sneaking in where no one, Raul, Mateo, or anyone else would see her. She didn't even turn the lights on, but tiptoed to the cupboard that hung over the countertop where she usually prepared and clipped live flowers, next to the flower cooler.

Pausing, she crossed her fingers and said a silent prayer. *Please, let them be there. They have to be there.*

She pulled the door open and reached in. It was too dark to see, so she groped for the plastic bag she had put them in. There. She touched it. She pulled it out.

Her knees felt weak as she felt the weight of the bag. Something was in it. When she reached inside and pulled out a plastic Whoopie Pie, her knees gave way with relief and she had to catch herself on the edge of the counter with both hands. The bag dropped to the floor.

She heard a sound at the rear of the shop. Had she left the door unlocked? Probably. She had intended to go right back out. Footsteps sounded, coming toward her.

Trying to stay still and undetected in that spot, so close to the counter where Raul had been preparing lilies, was a mistake. Lilies were one of her worst allergies. Her throat started to tickle and her nose to itch.

She stifled her sneeze as long as she could while the unknown person kept creeping slowly through the silence in her direction. The intruder was making barely audible noises, probably the friction of the person's clothing. The sounds drew closer. She cast about in her mind for a weapon, getting more frantic by the second. Her flower shears weren't within reach. Could she bop someone on the head with the bag of weighted fake candy pieces?

Then it happened. She gave a mighty sneeze.

The footsteps fled, the back door slammed. She was alone in the shop, holding a bag worth thousands of dollars. She couldn't leave it here. Whoever had just come for it would return. Was it Raul? The intruder had been heading straight for where she was, in front of the cupboard that held the hidden contraband.

Her first thought was to stuff the bag into her purse, but it wouldn't fit. She had to get out of there. She headed for the back door.

No. That's where the intruder had come from. What if he was out there? Waiting for her to exit so he could...what? Knock her down and take the jade?

Her mind felt heavy and dull. It was hard to think. She took a deep, slow breath.

She had to go out the front.

What if the intruder was there instead?

She called Tally.

14

Tally looked at her phone screen and wondered why Yolanda was calling her right now. They had just parted, less than half an hour ago. Yolanda should be heading to her parents' house for their Saturday dinner very soon.

"I can't hear you," Tally said. "Why are you whispering?" She hoped this wasn't an emergency. She was so tired and so comfy on the couch, her shoes kicked off, warm and rumbly Nigel snuggled in her lap, and a glass of lemonade at her fingertips.

"Can you drive to the back of my shop? Please? It's urgent."

She had gone to her shop! If she had told Tally she was going, Tally would have gone with her. Yolanda sounded scared. Tally dumped Nigel, stuck her glass in the fridge so Nigel wouldn't knock it over—ignoring some urgent, loud, feline complaints—stepped into her shoes, tore to her car, and drove off for the alleyway.

When Tally got there, Yolanda ran out, locked her door, and jumped into Tally's little two-door car.

"Did you see anyone in the alley?" Yolanda asked, swiveling her head to scan the surroundings.

She looked awfully worried. Panting like she'd just run a mile, she thrust a plastic bag into Tally's lap.

"What's—" Tally glimpsed the contents. Shiny plastic Whoopie Pies, pieces of fudge, some Mary Janes and Mallomars, and a couple of yellow, glowing Twinkies. She knew what they were. "These are the ones you haven't used in the window yet." Yolanda had gone back for them tonight.

"And never will, I think. Feel how heavy they are."

Tally lifted the bag. "Now we know why, don't we? I think it feels like these are full of jade, too. I would probably have thought they were weighted, silly me. To make them more stable, to stay in place better."

"They are weighted. They're still full of jade."

"Did you notice this before? When you were decorating and putting them in your window?"

"I didn't. Raul arranged them."

Tally pondered that, her mind stilling. Did that mean that Raul knew they were stuffed with contraband? She mentally shook her head. No, he might just think they were made of heavy plastic. Or, as they just said, weighted. Maybe.

"So you went to get these just now, right? Why didn't you have me go with you? What happened?"

"Someone came in while I was there. I scared them off, but I was afraid they were after these and they would kill me."

"Who was it? How many?"

"Just one person, I'm pretty sure. I just heard one set of footsteps, but I couldn't tell who it was. I had left the lights out. I didn't want anyone to see me in there getting these."

"Good thinking." Tally started driving out of the alley. "How did you scare him off?"

"I, um... I sneezed. He didn't expect anyone to be there, I'm pretty sure. Go slow," Yolanda said, peering out the window. "I want to see if whoever it was is still here."

"Waiting for you, you mean. That's why you wanted me to come get you. We have to take these to Jackson. Did you think the person sounded like Raul?"

"I couldn't tell. It couldn't be Raul, though."

"Why not?"

"Why would he sneak in here to get these? He's here all day. He could grab them whenever he wants."

That made sense. Tally handed the bag back to Yolanda and dipped her phone out of her pocket. The detective didn't answer his phone. "Should I leave a message?"

"Maybe," Yolanda said. "I can get to the police station at eight or so tomorrow morning. I'm so late for dinner right now. My father is going to be so upset."

Tally left a message telling Jackson she and Yolanda would be at the station in the morning and drove Yolanda home. They both looked carefully all along the way, but no one was lurking or acting suspicious. No one paid any attention to them driving by. Tally made sure Yolanda was inside before she took off. She kept the bag so that if anyone *was* watching, they wouldn't see Yolanda with it.

Before she could fall asleep, Tally wrestled with the idea of Raul being involved with the smuggling—and with Lily.

* * * *

Thet had been following Mateo for a few hours and was sure the young man didn't know he was there. Neither Ira nor Kyle, the housebreakers, had the missing jade. They didn't seem to know anything at all about any jade. They were just interested in watches, electronics, women's jewelry, and loose money.

Walter was sure they had possession of all the jade there was, all that was in the window. He assured Thet there was no more, but Thet knew differently. His original contact, Mateo, was the logical person to be holding some of it back. Yes, Sutton had tried to steal the bulk of it, but it was logical to think that Mateo had filched some of it from Sutton. Just a few pieces were worth a lot of American dollars.

So he followed Mateo, starting at noon. He went out to lunch and had a hamburger. Then he went back home and, Thet could see through the window, watched television and drank beer for a few hours.

Thet was just beginning to think he wouldn't go anywhere else, when he came out of his small house at nine in the evening. Hanging back was easy, even easier than it had been earlier, since Mateo was quite drunk by now. He staggered along the sidewalk, heading for downtown, for Main Street.

When he ducked into an alley, Thet worried he might not be able to go there without being seen, but Mateo never looked back. He lurched down the alley to the back door of a shop. If Thet wasn't mistaken, it was Bella's Baskets, the place the jade had been delivered to, then stolen from by Sutton. Before he took it from him in the motel.

Mateo fumbled a key in the lock and finally got the door open.

Of course! The rest of the jade was still in the shop! Thet should have thought of that. They had probably not used all of it in their display. He squeezed his eyes shut and rapped himself on the head for his stupidity. If he'd thought of that earlier, he would have all of his property by now.

All he had to do was wait until Mateo came out with it, then take it from him.

He wasn't inside for more than a minute, though, when he came running out. Mateo stopped to lock the door, then ran down the alley toward Thet.

Thet tried to stop him, but Mateo stuck out his arm and knocked the man over, an expression of fright on his face.

Thet sat in the alley, catching his breath from the blow to his chest. The jade must still be in the shop. Mateo had looked spooked, frightened. He didn't think Mateo had gotten the jade. What had scared him away? Thet would love to go inside and look for it. But he had seen Mateo lock it and had no way of getting in without breaking the door. He wasn't ready to do that, even if he could. And maybe what he wanted wasn't there. No, he wouldn't take that risk for something that might not even be there.

* * * *

When Yolanda drove up to the house, no one was outside. They had probably finished the cocktails long ago. She steeled herself for an icy reception and got out of her car, slamming the door harder than she intended to.

Just inside the front door, she heard a buzz of conversation. There were a lot of people in the house tonight.

Her mother called out from the living room. "Yolie? Is that you? Where have you been?"

There was no way she was going to worry them by telling them about what had just happened at her shop. She entered the living room and halted. Six of her eight cousins were there, standing, sitting on the couch, leaning on the mantel, all holding drinks and all staring at her.

"Now we can eat," her oldest cousin, Viggo said. "Cousin Yo decided to drop in, after all."

"We're starving," Viggo's sister Angela whined. "And where is this guy we're supposed to meet?"

"Guy?" Yolanda was confused, then the fog cleared. Her parents had invited the cousins to meet Kevin tonight. Steaming inside, she held her face in check and debated whether she should storm out now, or endure the insufferable company of her family tonight. She didn't like a single one of her cousins, and they had never liked her.

Suffering won out after she played through the consequences of leaving.

She put on her sweetest smile and aimed it at her mother. "I'm sorry? You thought I was bringing someone to dinner?"

Slight frown lines appeared between her mother's well-maintained eyebrows. "Kevin. The young man you're dating. The one you told us about."

"He's busy tonight."

"Next week?" her father asked.

"No, Papa, I don't think so."

The consequences of staying for dinner turned out to be only marginally better than those of storming out.

She was seated next to Angela, who wasted no time needling her cousin. "How's Violetta doing? I haven't seen her in ages."

Yolanda pasted on a bright smile. "She's great. Living in Dallas. Has a terrific job. Loves it there."

"Is she seeing anyone?"

Yolanda thought fast. Angela obviously knew about Vi's girlfriend and wanted to bring up the subject at the table. Yolanda wasn't having any of that. "She is. They're extremely happy. Are you dating anyone?"

Angela was notoriously hard on boyfriends. She'd never had one stick around for more than six months.

"How long ago was…Alvin? Alfred?" Yolanda asked with an innocent look.

Angela frowned. "That wasn't his name."

She didn't bring up Yolanda's sister again, at least.

When Yolanda left, early, she was careful not to storm out, but to merely leave. She felt her father's dark look following her out the front door. He hadn't said a word to her all night. There were probably some other daggers being stared at her back, but she didn't turn around to look.

* * * *

Sunday morning, Tally picked Yolanda up and they drove to the station. They got in to see Jackson Rogers right away.

"What's going on? Why did you have to see me first thing Sunday morning?" he asked.

Tally wondered if he was annoyed. He sounded like it. "Look." She held the bag out, opened up so he could see inside.

He took the bag and started taking out the contents. After the third one, he whistled. "Do all of these have smuggled Burmese jade in them?"

The women both nodded. "I think so," Tally said. "They must, right?"

Jackson twisted one. It was sturdy, not having been exposed to sunlight in the display window. He kept twisting until it broke apart at the seam and the brilliant green stones spilled onto his desk. He whistled again.

"I feel so awful about this," Tally said. "You said the people in Myanmar are suffering because of this jadeite." She couldn't take her eyes off the beautiful stones. "They really are pretty." She reached out to pick one up. It felt cool, smooth, and very solid.

He fingered the green stones. Then he inspected one of the whole plastic pieces that he hadn't broken apart yet. "These were put there during manufacturing. They couldn't have been inserted later." He ran a finger along the factory-sealed seam.

Tally could also see that the plastic seams were intact. The smuggling was being done where they were made, in Myanmar. That's where it started from. Mateo wasn't ever in Myanmar. He drove a warehouse truck—did he work for the smuggling company? Or the trucking company?

"Tell me," he asked. "Why was it so urgent you bring these in now?"

"Tell him," Tally said to Yolanda.

"I overheard a conversation. I thought it sounded like they knew there was more somewhere. More jade, I assumed. And they talked about being in danger, danger from some people who would kill them."

Jackson shook his head. "Yolanda, what are you talking about? Who did you overhear?"

Yolanda's dark eyes brimmed with tears. "It's Raul. My Raul. I can't believe it. I trust him completely. But the jade was in my shop, where he works every day."

"Raul and...who else?"

"He was talking to Mateo. On the phone. His cousin."

Jackson closed his eyes and breathed out audibly. "Tell me, if you can remember, exactly what they said."

"I only heard Raul."

He shook his head again. "Yes, okay. Can you tell me what Raul said?" Tally could tell he was holding onto his patience with difficulty. She also knew Yolanda didn't want to say what she had to. It looked so bad for Raul.

"Raul was...um...they were talking about needing money. About everyone needing money. Mateo, I think, wants Raul to ask me to hire him. Or maybe for Raul to ask for a raise. I can't do either of those things right now, though. Raul knows that."

"Raul told him that."

"Yes. Then I think Mateo must have said he was worried because Raul said that Mateo didn't kill Sutton so 'they can't get you for that.' But then—then he said..." She stopped and gave one short sob of distress. "He said to keep quiet and 'they' won't find out who's doing the smuggling."

Yolanda's shoulders shook and she sobbed softly. Tally handed her a tissue from her purse and put a hand on her quivering shoulder. "I was going to tell Raul to talk to you today if he knows the victim. I'm sorry I told you about this before I've had a chance to see him."

"It seems," Jackson said, "the Fuentes cousins are part of the smuggling ring."

"No!" Yolanda almost came out of her chair. "Y'all can't think that Raul is. It's his cousin. His cousin is part of it. I think he's protecting his cousin."

"I think," Jackson said, his voice steady as steel, "you're protecting Raul."

Tally felt the air go dark and heavy around them.

15

Tally drove a dispirited Yolanda back to start her day's work at Bella's Baskets.

"Now what?" Yolanda said, her voice flat and resigned. "Will Detective Rogers arrest Raul?"

They drove down Main Street, the cute shops with their cheerful displays contrasting with the low, lusterless spirits of both women.

"No, they won't arrest him," Tally said. "They don't have any evidence. Jackson won't arrest someone unless he has a good reason." She trusted him to do the right thing. He always had.

"So, what I told him isn't good enough?"

"I don't think so. Yo, it's just your word against his. If they want to question him, they will, but I don't see how Raul can be arrested because you overheard something."

Yolanda gave Tally an extremely doubtful look.

"You know what I think?" Tally said. "I think Mateo is in on it. For sure." She hesitated to say more.

"But not Raul?"

Tally told Yolanda no, but, in her heart, she wasn't at all positive about that. It looked very much like Raul *was* mixed up in the criminal activity. Two somber adages came to mind. One began with: If it looks like a duck. The other began: Where there's smoke. Neither one brought her any comfort.

* * * *

Yolanda got her chance to talk to Raul right away. After Tally dropped her off, Yolanda and Raul arrived at Bella's Baskets at the same time and came into the shop together. The smell of the lilies didn't seem so strong, but Yolanda could feel a tickle in her throat anyway.

Raul headed for the desk where the book of the day's orders was opened to today's date and started to sit down there, but Yolanda stopped him. "I need to tell you something, Raul."

"Sounds serious." He picked up the order book and started looking at it.

"I guess it is. Do you know—I mean, *did* you know—Sawyer Sutton? Know who he was?"

"Everybody knows him now, don't they? He's the dead guy at the motel." He took a seat at the desk, still looking at the book. "He's big news."

"I mean, did you know him before that?" She needed him to pay attention to her. Should she snatch the order book away?

Raul shook his head, bent to look more closely at the order book, then looked up. "You said you wanted to tell me something?"

Yolanda sucked her bottom lip into her mouth, trying not to chew on it. "I do."

After a few moments of silence, Raul prompted her. "And? What is it?"

"I happened to be in the police station and the detective asked me some questions."

His mouth fell open. "They're questioning *you*? They think *you* killed him?"

That made Yolanda smile. She couldn't help it. The thought was absurd. It felt good to use those facial muscles, at least, even if nothing was funny right now. "No, but…well, I told him I heard you mentioning the name on the phone, talking to your cousin."

Now she had his attention. He put down the order book and looked straight at her, something in his face. Fear? Apprehension? His voice was strained, but his words tumbled out. "They worked together, Mateo and Sawyer. He's afraid, since he didn't say he recognized who Sawyer was. In the motel room. He thinks the cops will think that's fishy. He doesn't know why he didn't say who it was. He knew right away. The door opened and he could see right away who it was. And that he was dead. He thinks that they might jump to some wrong conclusions."

"I imagine they might. Mateo worked with him. That's easy enough for them to find out. But you didn't know Sawyer Sutton, yourself?"

"Never met the guy. Never even heard of him before his name was in the news. Mateo never mentioned him. He didn't tell me much at all about that warehouse delivery job. I see why now, since it was on the shady side. He was being paid in cash."

Yolanda smiled in relief. "Just tell the detective what you told me if he wants to talk to you, okay?" If what Raul was saying was true, there was no danger of him being a part of the criminal acts.

"Sure." Raul hesitated.

"Did you want to tell me something else?" Yolanda asked. "Wait, I need to tell you what happened last night. I was in the shop and it was dark, the lights all turned off, so no one would have known I was here."

"Why were you here in the dark?" Raul smiled in his puzzlement.

"To tell the truth, I didn't want anyone to know I was here. I came in to get those extra plastic candies you had put in the cupboard. I had to take them to the police to see if they had smuggled jade in them. While I was here, someone else came in the back door to get them, I assume. But I already had them. I sneezed and scared the intruder away."

"That's…that's what I wanted to tell you. Mateo knew they were there. He was here when I put them away. If he knew they had the smuggled jewels in them, it could have been him. He wouldn't ever hurt you. I hope you know that." He paused again, then continued. "And one more thing I need to tell you. I don't have my shop key. I don't know what happened to it, but I think Mateo might have taken it."

Yolanda felt the tension leave her body. She was glad it hadn't been Raul. "I'll leave it alone for now. He didn't steal anything or hurt anyone. Thanks for telling me that." She should get the locks changed. Soon.

Raul went back to lining up the jobs for the day.

Yolanda hoped Raul was being truthful and wasn't just a good liar. She didn't think he'd ever lied to her. Why would he now? Okay, there were reasons. But she very much wanted to believe in him.

* * * *

When Lily came into Tally's Olde Tyme Sweets, soon after Tally's arrival, Tally stared at her so long and so often, trying to decide whether to talk to her or not, that Lily started giving her exasperated looks.

"What?" she said. "Are my clothes inside out? Is my head on backwards?"

Tally made up her mind. Yes, she had to say something. "Lily, I have to tell you something."

Lily had been preparing to do some candy making. They retreated to the corner of the kitchen with the reading chair. Tally motioned Lily into the soft chair and she sat on the footstool in front of her. Where should she start?

"What's going on between you and Raul?"

Lily narrowed her eyes. "We're dating."

"How serious are you?"

"Is that your business?" Lily sounded surprised that Tally would ask her that.

"I know, I know. It shouldn't be. But I know you want to stop rooming with your cousin, right?"

Lily nodded slightly, a suspicious look stealing over her face.

"And you and Raul seem perfect together."

Lily broke out into a sunny smile. "Oh, so you think I should move in with him? Is that what you wanted to tell me? That's so sweet of you. We are thinking about it. I'm glad you approve."

Lily jumped up, gave Tally a hug, and hurried into the bathroom, the one place Tally couldn't follow her.

Tally was stunned by Lily's conclusion and hadn't been able to think of what to say quickly enough. That hadn't gone the way it was supposed to. She would try later to get Lily to hold off on moving in with him, which was what she had wanted to suggest.

"Ms. Holt," Molly called from the front.

They were probably getting busy. Tally reluctantly left for the salesroom, leaving Lily in the bathroom for now. She would have to try talking to her about Raul being under suspicion later.

Tally's morning dragged into the afternoon with her expecting a call or text from Yolanda at any minute about Raul being taken in for questioning. She thought that what Yolanda told Jackson *was* enough grounds to do that. One minute she hoped he would get questioned so he could make it clear that he had nothing to do with the theft or the smuggling. The next minute thought she was being overly optimistic about the chances of that.

She wasn't able to grab another minute alone with Lily to try to clear up their misunderstanding. Lily practically bounced through the day, glowing, giving Tally happy, secret looks every once in a while. Tally groaned inwardly every time and returned a weaker smile.

To make her day even worse, the woman who had accused Dorella of wearing her jewelry came in for some Mary Janes. She asked to see Dorella as Lily was ringing her up.

"I'm sorry, it's Ms. Diggs's day off," Lily said, being cool and polite. Tally was proud of her. "Would you like to leave a message for her?"

The woman sniffed. "I just wanted to see if she's wearing any more of my jewelry. I'm missing a pearl necklace. Double strand. I've reported it to the police." The woman snatched her package and walked out, slamming the door so hard that the usually soft chimes clattered and jangled.

"If that woman breaks my chimes…" Tally muttered to herself.

Lily broke into a laugh. "I can't imagine Dorella wearing a double strand of pearls. That's something our grandparents would wear, right?"

Molly grinned, agreeing with her.

Tally wasn't so sure. She happened to like pearls. She didn't own any, but might wear them if she had them. And she was nowhere near the age to be Lily's grandmother. She was a bit older than either Lily or Dorella, but not that much.

A few hours later, Tally gratefully flipped the sign to *closed* and locked the front door. "Okay, let's clean up."

Molly started sweeping the floor in the front and Lily carried the unsold goods back to the kitchen to put into the refrigerator, while Tally took the proceeds out of the cash register to count in the office. Before she could leave the room, Dorella appeared at the front door. She tried the locked door, rattling the knob, then knocked.

Molly ran to open the door. "Come to help with the dirty work?" Molly kidded her.

Dorella stepped in, dressed in a glamorous low-cut black dress, silver heels, her soft blond curls swept into an updo, clutching a pearl-studded evening bag. And wearing a double-strand pearl choker.

"Oh my." Molly dropped the broom to the floor with a thud.

Tally clanged the money drawer down onto the glass-topped display case. "Dorella. Where did you get those pearls?"

Dorella put her left hand to her throat, looking slightly puzzled at both of them. "They're nice, aren't they?" She smiled as she stroked them. "I never had pearls before. They feel so cool and smooth."

Tally repeated, "Dorella, where did you get them?"

She grinned. "Ira gave them to me yesterday. We're going out to an extra-fancy dinner tonight. He said he did some work for a guy and got a nice paycheck."

"Stay here for a minute." Tally ran into the office to call Jackson on her cell, avoiding eye contact with Lily, who was in the kitchen. "You need to come over here. Right now," she said when he answered. "Quick."

Tally turned around after ending the call to find Dorella at her office door.

"What are you doing, Tally? What's wrong with these pearls?" Her eyes were worried and a little hostile.

Tally slumped, resting her hip on her desk. "You remember that woman who accused you of having her ring?"

Tally heard a siren in the distance, drawing closer. She tried not to react, not to flinch.

"That old biddy? I sure do. I couldn't believe it. How could she— Wait." Dorella touched the pearls again and cocked her head toward the front, hearing the siren, too. "Who did you just call?"

"She was in here earlier today, Dorella. She said someone had stolen her pearls."

Dorella's eyes opened wide. "So you automatically think Ira stole them?" She spun and stalked through the kitchen, headed for the front door.

Detective Jackson Rogers came through the door just before Dorella reached it. "What's this about, Ms. Holt?" he asked, glancing at Dorella, then looking past her while blocking her exit.

Tally assumed he was being formal, calling her "Ms. Holt" in front of her staff. "Well…" She tilted her head toward Dorella, focusing her eyes on Dorella's neck from behind her.

Jackson squinted at both of them, then it dawned on him. "Yes. I see. Ms. Diggs, I have to ask you a few questions."

Dorella stomped her right foot. Tally was afraid she might snap off the pretty silver heel. "What's wrong with you people? Ira gave this to me. He's not stealing that horrible woman's jewelry."

Jackson used his softest, calmest voice. "I understand. I just need to verify a few things."

"I'm not going to the police station. I'll be late."

"We can talk here."

Tally piped up. "You can use my office." She turned her head away so she wouldn't see the look Dorella gave her as she passed by.

Molly, still standing where she'd been when she dropped the broom, bent to pick it up and continued sweeping. Lily appeared from the kitchen, also wide-eyed.

"What's going on?" Lily asked. "Is Detective Rogers arresting Dorella?"

"No, no," Tally said. "I'm not sure what's going on. But someone, or several someones, have been breaking into people's houses and stealing things."

"Dorella?" Lily asked, incredulous. "Not Dorella."

"I seriously doubt it. But that new boyfriend of hers, Ira Mann…he's given her two things that one of our customers says are hers, jewelry that was stolen from her."

Lily shook her head. "Oh man. Poor Dorella. She needs to go back to dating your brother."

Tally smiled, in spite of the tension she felt. "I think you're right."

When Jackson emerged twenty minutes later, he looked grim. After he left, Dorella came from the kitchen, without the pearls. Her chin trembled with the effort to keep from crying. "He thinks Ira's a burglar. He thinks Ira's robbing people. That's crazy. Ira is on the crime watch. He's a Crime Fritzer, one of the good guys. He's trying to keep those robbers out of everyone's houses."

But wouldn't that be a handy position to be in? Keeping watch over the neighborhood houses, pretending to protect them, while also being the very person stealing from them. "The detective will get it all straightened out."

"What if he doesn't? What if he arrests Ira?"

"He can't arrest him unless he has a reason."

"He *has* a reason. Reasons." Dorella's voice rose and tears spilled down her cheeks. "False accusations. But they're reasons."

Tally handed her a tissue from the box behind the counter.

"Can I use your office a minute more?" Dorella asked. "I have to call Ira." She dashed back through the kitchen and Tally heard her slam the office door.

"Should she do that?" Lily said. "Should she warn him like that?"

"I'm not sure," Tally said. "Probably not. But I'm not going to wrestle her." She wondered why Dorella didn't use her own phone. So the police would never know she warned him?

Dorella still needed to fix her makeup, Tally observed, as the young woman left after her call. The pearls had worked perfectly with her ensemble. Her neck looked bare.

Lily hurried through her tasks, probably because she was meeting Raul, and left before Tally and Molly, for once. Molly hadn't talked about any of this, but Tally could tell she was thinking about it, mulling things over in her mind.

"What do you think, Ms. Holt?" she asked as they both untied their smocks and hung them on the pegs.

"I think there are a lot of possibilities, but I don't know anything for sure."

"Like it's possible Dorella's new boyfriend is a burglar?"

"That's one."

"Like Dorella is a burglar?"

"No, that isn't one. I don't think that." Molly started out the door. "You shouldn't think that, either."

"I guess not. I have to work with her." Molly stopped in the doorway, holding it open. "I think something good is going to happen."

"For you?" Tally hoped that was true, although she hoped it wasn't a better job somewhere and hoped she wouldn't lose Molly as an employee. Although that would not be a bad thing for Molly.

"It's my dad. Howie has been talking to him."

"What about?"

Molly seemed reluctant to impart her news. "Well, I'm just not sure. But Howie thinks Dad could teach auto mechanics."

"Of course he could! What a great idea. Has your dad talked to anyone?"

"No, and he hasn't said he wants Howie to talk to anyone, either."

"Would he be teaching in high school?"

"No, junior college. The hours are better. Well, less."

"Good luck getting him to consider that. I think it would be great."

Molly left with a big grin on her face. More income in her family would certainly ease the pressure on the poor young woman.

* * * *

When Tally got home that night, she stewed for at least an hour before calling her brother. It was late in Texas, but it was earlier in Tucson, where he was doing his current sculpture installation.

"Have you heard from the 'rents?" he asked.

"They're fine for now, I think. They're in Rome, I'm pretty sure. But Dorella isn't fine."

"Now what? I just spoke with her yesterday. She's still in tight with Ira. She seemed all right."

"Did she mention a gift of pearls?"

"Pearls? Old lady pearls?"

Tally had to snicker. She would have to give a lot of thought before ever wearing pearls. "That's exactly what they are. And this time they are probably stolen from the same women Ira took the ring from."

"Oh, Dorella. What are you doing? Talk to her, Sis. She has to quit that guy."

"I'm with you there. I can't tell her that, though. He's probably being arrested, so maybe that will do it."

"You know what? I'm finishing up here in another couple of days. Maybe I should come up there and sweep her off her feet."

"Again."

"I'll do it for real. For keeps. I've been missing her. A lot."

Just before Tally climbed into bed, she got a call from her dad's phone. Nigel was already in position, next to her pillow, warming up the sheets for her.

"Dad? Everything okay? You got to Rome okay?"

He huffed into the phone. That didn't sound good.

"Dad? You there?"

"Yes, I'm here. Sorry. Just barely. Your mother and I are being detained."

"Detained? What does that mean? Who is detaining you?"

"We were taken aside going through customs in Rome. At first I couldn't figure out what the problem could be. They went through our luggage, but that's not uncommon. We carry some unusual items for our acts. Costumes that could, I suppose, look like disguises."

"Are you okay now?"

"No, I'm not!"

Oh dear. Something was very wrong. Tally made her voice smooth and calming. "Tell me what's going on."

"Your mother and I are in jail cells in Rome. If I figured it out correctly—my Italian isn't awfully good and no one here speaks English—the customs people think we're trying to smuggle something."

Tally, who had been standing next to her bed, plopped down onto it. Nigel sprang up and jumped to the floor, looking offended. "Smuggling? Really? What do they think you're smuggling?"

He gave a weary sigh. "I can't for the life of me figure that out. They took my satchel, then they grabbed all of Nancy's stage jewelry and tossed it in a bag. Although that seemed like an afterthought."

"They couldn't think her jewelry is real, could they? It only looks good from the audience, as I recall."

"I bought your mother a nice piece in Gibraltar. It's a clear quartz ring. Not cheap, but not a diamond, which is what they thought it was. I can't find the receipt for it. But they don't seem too concerned about that."

Tally pictured the satchel he always carried, his man-purse, she always called it. He always objected to that term. "They took your satchel first? What all is in it?"

"Just the usual things. Some papers. Our schedules, contracts. Extra cash. All of our records."

"Dad, that satchel is awfully old. You have things in there from years ago, don't you? Can you think of anything that would look suspicious? I mean, that would appear that way, even when it's not?"

"How could my satchel look suspicious?"

"What else was in it?"

"Well, some snacks. A couple of apples, some grapes, a bag of doughnuts from the airport."

"Do they have rules about not bringing in food?"

"If they do, they just confiscate the food and throw it out. They don't toss us in the slammer, Tally. This is insane!"

She had to agree with him. Something was going on that she and her dad and mom hadn't figured out yet.

After they cut off the call, she went back over everything he had said. Papers. Apples, grapes, and doughnuts. And her mother's new ring. They couldn't think they were smuggling that. They would have a receipt. She wanted to see it. Maybe they could send a picture when they were…free.

Tally slept in Monday morning, the one day a week her shop was closed. It wasn't to be a day of rest for her, though. She had lain awake fretting for hours about her parents before her worries turned to Dorella. It would make perfect sense for Ira, and possibly a few others, to be breaking into the houses they were supposed to be protecting, but she hoped, over and over, that it would turn out not to be true.

She stumbled to her kitchen and poured kibble for Nigel, who had been patiently—for a cat—meowing and batting her face at least half an hour. After making a batch of coffee and some toast, she turned on the television in her living room and got a local channel. In a crawler across the bottom of the screen of the morning talk show was the *Breaking News* flash she had dreaded.

Son of Fredericksburg fire chief arrested as part of burglary ring. More arrests expected. Address from the Fire Chief Mann at 10:00 this morning.

That was an hour yet. Poor Mr. Mann. At least it didn't look like he was part of the "ring," since he wasn't arrested. Yet. Just his son. What on earth would he say?

She heard her phone ringing in the bedroom where she'd left it. She ran in to see that her parents were calling here again. It was her dad's phone.

"Dad! Are you free now?"

"We are not." His voice was hoarse, weary. He would never be able to perform this way.

"Is anything going on? Have they told you anything?"

"They questioned both of us for hours and hours about some powder."

"Powder? Like…drugs?"

"That has to be what they're thinking. But I have no idea what they're talking about. They showed me a little bit of powder in a plastic bag. They say it came from my satchel."

"Do you know what it is?"

"Of course not!" She had made him indignant. "I don't carry white powder around with me."

"Oh dear, do you suppose someone planted it on you?"

"Now you sound melodramatic, dear. No one planted anything. I've had the bag with me all the time. They swear it was in with my things."

Tally started pacing the room, wondering what would be their defense if someone had actually snuck the powder into her dad's luggage. Maybe they could test it for fingerprints.

"Are your fingerprints on the plastic bag? Have they looked at that?"

"Tally, is wasn't all in the bag. Some of it was loose in the bottom."

That was just too strange. She heard someone telling her dad to cut off the call. She stood still for a moment trying hard to think. She was concentrating so hard, she ignored her phone, before gradually realizing it was ringing. Dorella was calling her. With more than a little trepidation, knowing this was another crisis, she answered it.

"Tally," Dorella wailed. "They've arrested Ira! They really did!"

"Have you talked to him?"

"He called me from the jail just now. I wonder if they questioned him all night. Can they do that?"

"I don't know." *Probably.* "Did they pick him up last night? What did he say?"

"He said—he said—" She broke down sobbing.

"Do you want me to come over?" Tally asked. This was too hard over the phone.

"No." Dorella cut the call off.

Was she angry with Tally for calling the detective? She certainly had every right to be. But there had to be a reason Ira had been arrested, more than just Dorella wearing jewelry that resembled the stolen items. It was becoming more apparent that her suspicions had been right. When she tried to call Dorella back, it went to voice mail. She took a deep breath and poured herself another cup of coffee.

It was almost ten by then, Tally realized. She rinsed her toast plate and knife and carried the cup of coffee into her living room. She turned on the television to see the public announcement by the fire chief. What could he possibly say?

She perched on the edge of the couch and soon learned. Not much.

He started by congratulating the police for investigating the string of home burglaries. No mention of an arrest. No mention of his son, Ira. He acted like the breaking news had never happened. He went on to talk about the tremendous progress the city leaders were making and ended by hoping the danger to the citizens of "our fair city" would soon feel safer.

That was one way to deal with embarrassing relatives, Tally guessed. Just ignore them. The problem here was that this made the chief look complicit. Like he was covering something up. She expected Dorella to call about it, but her phone remained silent.

After a shower and getting dressed, with still no more word from Dorella, Tally dallied with the idea of going to see her, but decided instead to go look in on Mrs. Gerg. Maybe she'd stop at Dorella's after that. Give her time to get herself together. Or to finish falling apart.

16

Yolanda paced her small living room, almost wearing a rut in the thin, expensive area rug in front of her brocade couch. Tomorrow, Tuesday, she would be back at work. Raul would be, too. Maybe. She had to decide how to act toward him. Her first choice would be... well, normal. To act like he hadn't scared the daylights out of her by trying to steal the remaining jade-filled fake candies. But no, of course he hadn't. Had he? She didn't know for sure who the intruder had been. It could very well have been Mateo.

Was Raul involved in this whole mess? Smuggling jade? Intercepting the route to steal it? Then trying again to steal it when the interception went wrong? Or was it all Mateo? If Mateo was even involved.

The tension, working with Raul on Sunday, had been intense. He briefly mentioned that the police had talked to him the night before, but didn't offer up any more information about that, other than to ask her if she was okay, after someone crept into the place to—maybe—steal the jade while she was there, cowering on the floor.

She had sent him out on errand after errand to avoid talking to him about any of it, since she didn't know what to say, what to think. At the end of the day she had enough ribbon, tissue paper, and plastic overwrap to last at least three months. Raul hadn't complained about all the unnecessary trips, but had started giving her funny looks.

On Monday, the day Bella's Baskets was closed, Yolanda had lunch with Kevin. She didn't mention the events of Saturday night. She wasn't sure why. Maybe it was because Kevin was already fully convinced she should fire Raul, just because he was related to Mateo. Was she afraid Kevin would talk her into doing it?

She wasn't looking forward to Tuesday morning one little bit. Halting in her frantic circuit around the living room, she plopped into her wingback chair and let her head loll against the right-hand wing. There was only one thing to do. She would have to bring everything out into the open. There would have to be a conversation with Raul. This quiet suspicion couldn't go on. She couldn't take the tension.

* * * *

On Monday Tally busied herself during the day with errands and housework, putting everything else off. When her father called her in the afternoon, she pounced on the phone. She hadn't called them, thinking maybe it would be better to let them call her. She didn't know if they were still being detained and probably couldn't call them if they were.

This time it was her mom. "Tally, you'll never guess what it was."

Tally had been unloading the dishwasher and immediately started drumming her fingers on the kitchen counter. "I'm sure you're right. Can you tell me?" At least her mother sounded happy, not distraught. "Are you out of jail?"

"Yes, finally. You father had bought doughnuts. Powdered sugar doughnuts."

Tally's mouth fell open and her fingers stopped moving. "Did no one think to taste the powder?"

"I did," her mother said proudly. "I finally told them, I'd taste it. They had done tests for all kinds of drugs and it wasn't anything. It flaked off those doughnuts. They were actually kind of stale when he bought them. It's no wonder all the powdered sugar fell off into the bag."

"Are you free to go?"

"Yes. We're gone. I mean, we're out of the jail building. On our way to the hotel. Finally. Now the show can go on, if the venue still has us booked."

She knew that was the most important thing to them. The show, of course, must always go on. What a mess her parents had gotten into. Other people didn't have to worry about their parents the way she and Cole did, she was sure. Cole hadn't even shared in this latest crisis. To spare him, she hadn't told him any of the Powdered Sugar Crisis, as she would always think of it. She would tell him eventually, now that she could laugh about the whole incident.

She walked to Mrs. Gerg's early Monday evening instead of driving, to use up some of her nervous energy. A white van that said *Arlen's Aqua Shop* on the side in blue letters was parked in front of Mrs. Gerg's house, shining in the light from the streetlamp. She had seen it before. Was it Walter's? It had a Dallas phone number under the lettering. She had no idea what kind of car Walter drove. But was he able to drive now? No, it was much too soon. The car could have belonged to someone visiting a neighbor, even though it was directly in front of Mrs. Gerg's front porch. The spaces in front of both the neighboring houses were full.

She mounted the porch steps and tapped on the door. No one answered, but she could hear voices inside. Male voices. She knocked harder. Should she have called?

The door was flung open by the short Asian man she had seen here before with the cowboy. She had only glimpsed his face What was his name? She could never remember it. It didn't seem to fit him.

"Hi," she said. "Remember me? Tally Holt?"

He frowned, but stepped aside so she could come in.

She stood her ground for a moment. "Your name is...Thought?"

"Thet," he said. So it was the same man.

"Oh yes. Nice to see you again. Is Mrs. Gerg here?" The whole name came tumbling back to her, Thet Thura. The other man was there, too, the one with the boots, his hat resting on his knee. Yes, his name was Arlen. That was his van outside.

Thet took another step back and she walked into the house. That must be his van out front, she thought, unless it belonged to the other man. Arlen looked up at Tally from the couch and said, "Howdy," in a low, rasping voice. Probably from that chaw poking out his lip.

Mrs. Gerg sat on her sofa, huddled into the corner of it, a pinched, apprehensive look on her face. Thet glared at Mrs. Gerg for three full seconds before he stomped off into the kitchen. The lanky, tall man unwound from the couch and followed him, his boots clomping on the floor when he reached the tile floor in the kitchen. A reek of tobacco trailed after him. Tally thought Walter was probably there since he wasn't in the living room.

Tally sat next to Mrs. Gerg. "Are you doing okay?"

The woman nodded, but the worry didn't leave her face. Tally took her hands, noticing the bruises on her arms. She touched one lightly, looking her question at the older woman. Mrs. Gerg shook her head and darted her eyes toward the kitchen.

Tally leaned close. "I can help you. Do you want to come stay with me?"

"I can't," she whispered.

"Why not?"

Mrs. Gerg cast a forlorn look at the floor. "I just can't." Then she looked Tally in the eyes. "Everything will be fine." She attempted a smile. "This will be just fine in a little bit. I'll be fine." But her face remained worried-looking and her shoulders stayed hunched.

The voices in the kitchen were getting louder.

"It sure is!" a man shouted.

"It's not! That is not a knockoff. I can tell." That was Walter.

"Not so loud," Thet hissed.

"What are they doing?" Tally asked.

"They're…looking over some merchandise. Thet and Arlen are buying and selling things. With Walter."

She heard them speaking in low murmurs, the rasp of the cowboy coming through occasionally. "I came to see if I can get you anything," Tally said. "I have time to run to the grocery store if you'd like."

"No, we're okay."

Tally wanted to see what was going on in the kitchen. She stood. "I need a glass of water. Can I get one for you?"

Mrs. Gerg jumped up. "No! No, I don't need one. Please don't go in there. You should leave. Please leave."

Tally stepped very close, her voice low. "You'd better call me if you need anything. Okay?"

Mrs. Gerg nodded. She looked like she was on the verge of tears. "I will. You go now."

"Are you sure you're not in danger?"

"No, no danger."

Tally couldn't steal more than a glimpse into the kitchen as she left. But she clearly saw a mound of shiny objects on Mrs. Gerg's kitchen table. It looked like a pile of jewelry and watches. Maybe she had found more members of the house theft ring.

As she left, she looked at the van again. The man inside the house was Arlen, so this van was his—Arlen's Aqua Shop. And there was a Dallas phone number under the name.

17

Tally walked toward Dorella's apartment after leaving Mrs. Gerg with those two men, against her better judgment, but her phone rang before she got even halfway there.

"Tally, it's Jackson."

She was glad she had dithered around and hadn't eaten yet. They met at Rathskeller, both arriving at the same time and descending the stairway together.

They each had a glass of wine before ordering. Jackson said he wanted to decompress. "It's been a busy couple of days. More than a couple."

"You have a lot going on, don't you? You picked up Ira Mann for the break-ins, and you have a murder in the motel. Then there's the jade-smuggling."

"It's a lot, but it's all related."

"All of it?" The murder and the smuggling, yes, but the break-ins, too?

"I should say, it all ties together."

"There's more going on than you're telling me," Tally said, running her finger around the rim of the wineglass. The dry, deeply red liquid was hitting the spot tonight.

He gave her a wry one-sided smile. The one that scrunched up one of his eyes and made her heart leap a half an inch or so. "You know I can't tell you everything. Mateo finding the body of the guy who ran into his truck does seem to be a coincidence. But everything else ties together logically."

"So you don't think Mateo killed him?"

He clamped his lips together and gave her a pointed look. He wasn't going to say.

"Well, I think I found something related to the break-ins."

He leaned across the table, an earnest, worried expression on his handsome face. "Tally, don't go poking around in this business. It's not safe."

"I'm not poking around. I just saw it. By accident." It was kind of by accident. "And I want you to make sure Mrs. Gerg is okay."

"Tally, what are you talking about? What have you been up to?"

"I really did just want to check up on her. She didn't sound right on the phone."

"So you went over there."

"I did. And I have to tell you...what I saw."

"I'll bite. What did you see? When was it?"

"Those awful men were there just now, Thet Thura and Arlen somebody. They were in her kitchen with Walter and there was a pile of jewelry on the table. It looked like watches, rings, necklaces—"

"Just now?"

"Yes. Just a few minutes ago. I came directly here from there." Her fingers started drumming on the tabletop all by themselves.

"If Thura is involved...I have to go."

Tally bit her tongue to keep from saying that they hadn't eaten. She didn't think he would react so immediately. She sat on her hands to stop her fingers, but her knee decided to jiggle up and down instead.

He called dispatch before he left the table. She heard him ask for a quick warrant and for police officers to pick up Thura and Wright and the third man at Mrs. Gerg's house, and also to pick up Armand Mann. The fire chief.

"Wait just two seconds," Tally said. "I'm afraid for Mrs. Gerg. Could you make sure she's okay? And why are you picking up the chief?"

"He and Thura both have Dallas connections. Might as well question them both."

After he dashed off, taking the stairs up to the street level two and three at a time, Tally relaxed. With Walter and the two men, Thet and Arlen, out of there, Mrs. Gerg should be safer. And the fire chief. Could he be an old acquaintance of the mysterious men?

Her phone vibrated a second before it rang and she saw her dad's name. She grabbed it almost before it could make a sound.

"Dad! What's going on?"

"We're on our way to the Circus Maximus and our next performance. They're waiting for us to show up." She could tell he was smiling. There was a lift in his voice. "We thought they might cancel and replace us with another act. They actually did book someone else for these last few days, but now they want us to come perform."

"I'm so glad. How are your voices?" She'd been worried about that.

"We've both been doing vocal exercises. Your mom says she's one hundred percent and I'm almost there."

"You know, there's that ripped place in the lining of your satchel. You'd better check. Make sure nothing else is in there."

He laughed. "We'll do just that. For now, we have to run. Got shows to do."

At least that load was off her shoulders. She was glad she hadn't told Cole anything about this yet. He would have worried, and for nothing.

She had decided to forego her Monday night visit to Setting Sun, but she was free now, so she thought she might as well go there. It would take her mind off everything else.

Most of the residents, the ones who were still up, were watching TV in the communal room. She greeted everyone and the ones who could speak greeted her back. Some of them recognized her, some were just polite to everyone even though they couldn't tell who anyone was anymore. And a few were cranky. But those people were that way most of the time.

Tally took a seat on the couch with two women, one of whom was knitting what looked like an endless scarf.

"Very pretty," Tally said and the woman beamed.

A nurse entered the room with a tray of small paper pill cups. When she got to the knitter, Tally remembered what she had wanted to ask someone here. "Have you worked here long?" she asked the nurse, who had been there since Tally started visiting.

"I'd call it long," she said with a smile. "I started here fifteen years ago."

"Do you remember a janitor by the name of Walter?"

"What's his last name?" She fed the pills to the woman beside Tally and gave her a cup of water to wash them down.

"Wright. Walter Wright."

The nurse made a sour face. "Oh yes, I remember him. He got fired. Wasn't here very long."

"Can you tell me what he did?"

The nurse leaned down close. "I'm probably not supposed to. There are these rules about employment and confidentiality. But he's bad news. He was stealing from these people. Can you imagine? Cash and jewelry. Even wedding rings."

"Did you have him arrested?"

"No, no. We didn't want any trouble. He gave most of it back and we told him not to return."

Tally nodded. The pieces were falling into place.

18

Tally waited an hour before she called Mrs. Gerg to see where things stood after the police had presumably rounded up the three men. As she spoke on the phone, it felt like the woman didn't want to talk to Tally, evading her questions. Tally was as direct as she could be, to test a theory.

"Mrs. Gerg, are Walter and the other two men still at your house?"

"Almost," she said.

It seemed that they hadn't been arrested. Or taken in and released already? She understood that Mrs. Gerg couldn't talk freely so Tally would have to ask her questions she could answer with answering directly.

"Is Walter there?" she asked.

"Yes."

"Is Thet Thura there?"

"No, not at all."

She was playing along perfectly. "Did the police pick them up?"

"Definitely not."

"Why not? Okay, let me think how to ask you. Did the police find anything on your kitchen table when they got there?"

"No, nothing."

"Mrs. Gerg, I've found out something about Walter. He was fired from a job for stealing. You need to—"

"We're fine. I have to go now."

So. They were fine? Maybe she meant that the men had gotten rid of the evidence. Maybe Thet or Arlen had taken it with them. Had they fled out the back when the police showed up? Or did they coincidentally leave before they got there? She had a chilling thought. Would Walter blame

Mrs. Gerg for the raid? Would he hurt her badly? She wondered what had happened with the fire chief. Had they arrested him?

She didn't even try to call Jackson, figuring he must be very busy right now. She ate a late supper, made from throwing together things that were in her refrigerator, disappointed that she and Jackson hadn't gotten to have a nice meal at Rathskeller. Maybe some other time.

When the television news came on at ten, she was waiting for it, cat in lap, iced tea at her elbow. The broadcast only brought her more disappointment. There wasn't a single mention of any trouble at Mrs. Gerg's. Nothing about Walter Wright or any raids or arrests. And nothing about the fire chief. Jackson had said that Armand Mann and Thet Thura might be connected since the Manns were from Dallas.

Something pinged at the back of her mind, something to do with Thet and Dallas and Armand Mann. The offhand comment came back to her. Jackson had mentioned that both Armand Mann and Thura had Dallas connections, but that was it. Were they connected with each other? Or were they all connected to Arlen, who drove the van with the Dallas phone number? She would ask Jackson about that. Not that he would tell her anything, but she had to try.

* * * *

Yolanda had a better day at work on Tuesday than she thought she would. It started out with her and Raul facing each other on stools at the work counter.

"Raul, I need to know exactly what's going on. There's all kinds of speculation floating around." True, it was herself speculating, but still, Raul didn't need to know that.

"Rumors about what? What do you want to know? Lily and I are getting kind of serious."

Yolanda's mind paused. That wasn't what she'd been thinking about. "That's nice. I like her a lot."

Raul smiled a golden smile. "I do, too. I haven't ever liked anyone this much. What do you want to know? We don't have any plans right now. Yet."

"I wasn't thinking about Lily. I need to know about Mateo."

Raul looked puzzled. "What about him?"

"What exactly are his connections to what happened? To my window getting broken? And to the plastic being used for smuggling? I want to know the extent of his involvement."

Raul shook his head. "He worked in the place that's involved with the smuggling, yes, the place where they warehouse and ship the plastic that comes from Asia. I'm pretty sure he was planning on doing something illegal when he had the wreck that night."

"Did he know his truck was being used for transporting the smuggled jewelry stones?"

"I think so."

"Is there any connection with the home robberies? I need to know if he's involved. And if you are, too."

"Those break-ins? No, I'm not. I don't think he is, either. He said he was in the crime watch group and he's been bragging to me all the time that he's in on the burglary ring, but last night he told me he's not. Not really."

"What? What are you saying?"

"That some of the people in the crime watch group are the ones robbing the houses."

"Mateo is either in or he isn't. Which is it?"

"He knows who's involved, and he wants to join them. I tell him to stay away from that, but he doesn't listen to me. He's tried to get in on it, to join the people robbing the houses, but they don't tell him anything. He says they don't trust him."

"I wonder why," Yolanda said, twirling her hair around her finger. "How much do you need to trust a fellow thief?"

Raul smiled at that. "He fell asleep driving the truck and messed up somebody's plans. I don't know who was in on that, but I think no one trusts him now. Still, I don't think he had anything to do with the stealing from the houses."

Yolanda leaned forward. "So tell me. Who is in the theft ring?"

"He won't tell me. He still thinks they'll let him in."

"What about finding the dead guy in the motel?"

Raul shook his head. "Yeah, something was up with that. He knew who he was, but didn't tell the police. But the two of them were supposed to work together with the smuggling, him and Sawyer, so he acted like he didn't know him."

"Work together how?"

"He told me all of this after Sawyer Sutton died. Mateo was driving the company truck. He was supposed to meet Sawyer at night, on the way to Dallas, and stop the truck. Sawyer was going to intercept him and take the goods from him, like a holdup. A fake hijacking. And Mateo would say he was robbed and didn't know who did it. Then Sutton was supposed to pass the stuff to someone else the next day to take to a fish shop, or something, in Dallas. There was some kind of shipping mess-up and they were supposed to do that so the stuff got to the right destination. It wasn't labeled to go to Dallas. The smugglers messed up and wanted Mateo and Sawyer to fix the mess-up."

"And instead, Mateo crashed into his partner?"

"Broke Sawyer's leg. The shipping company has GPS on all the trucks, so they heard about the crash right away, and sent another truck to pick up the goods and deliver them to us, to Bella's Baskets. They didn't know it was stuff being smuggled and that it really shouldn't go here. They just went by the label."

"What are they smuggling?" Yolanda asked.

"He didn't even know at the time."

Yolanda gave a short laugh. "Your poor cousin. He's a terrible criminal. I wouldn't trust him, either."

"I know. He's not the brightest of my cousins."

Yolanda and Raul worked together much more easily that day. She was glad they had cleared the air. While still not 100 percent certain that Raul wasn't the crook that his cousin was, she was 99 percent convinced. Raul had never taken a dime from the shop. She trusted him with shopping, deliveries—everything, really. Just because his cousin was a bad one, didn't mean Raul was.

Later in the day she got a frantic call from Tally.

* * * *

Molly was in the kitchen dipping caramel-candy squares into chocolate and Lily was waiting on customers as Tally straightened the goods that customers had shifted. She sighed with pleasure. This was what she wanted, to work in her shop. To have the help of Molly and Lily, and Dorella, too. They were all good people. And to be left in peace to make her goodies and sell them. To make customers happy. Why did dark things have to intrude on her sunny days?

As she tried to push down the thoughts about dark things, her cell phone rang with a call that said it was from the hospital. Puzzled, she answered it. At first she couldn't understand the slurred gibberish of the person calling her, then the voice changed.

"This is Candace Gerg's nurse. Ms. Holt?"

"Nurse?"

"She's in the hospital. She's having trouble speaking from her injuries, but wants to talk to you."

Injuries? What now? "Okay. I'll try and understand her."

Mrs. Gerg got back on the phone, but Tally still couldn't make out what she was trying to say.

"Mrs. Gerg? I'm coming over there. Let me talk to the nurse again." She told the nurse she would be there in a few minutes.

First she called Yolanda. Her fingers shook as she pressed the keys. "Yo? Something's wrong with Mrs. Gerg. I'm afraid it might be my fault." She could feel her voice trembling.

"Whoa, slow down. Where are you?"

"I'm at the shop, but I'm going to the hospital to see her."

"The *hospital?*"

Tally rushed on. "I couldn't understand her over the phone."

"What do you mean, your fault? How can you put her in the hospital? Hey, take a deep breath. I can hear you panting."

Tally realized she was hyperventilating. She tried to slow her breathing. The remembered sight of those bruises on Mrs. Gerg's arms haunted her. She knew Walter Wright had hurt her.

She cut the call and told her employees she had to leave. It was a couple of hours until closing time.

"You can leave early if you want to, but I have an emergency I have to take care of."

"Is there anything I can do?" Lily asked, handing the customer her purchase and her receipt.

"No, nothing. Tell Molly, okay?"

Tally ran out the front door. She had walked to work and didn't have her car there. She ran most of the way home to get it. When she finally reached the vehicle, she wasted no time and jumped into her car.

19

Tally had gotten her car started and was beginning to back out of her driveway when Yolanda called. Tally stopped before she got into the street.

"Yes? I'm on my way to the hospital. I'll call you back, okay?"

"No, not okay! They've just taken Raul away."

Tally put the car in Park. "Who's they? Where did they take him?"

"To the police station. I think he's being arrested."

"For what?"

"I had just decided, just today, that he was innocent. That all the trouble was caused by his cousin and he had nothing to do with any of this mess. And now this."

"I'll call Jackson. Hang on."

She quickly punched the numbers for his cell phone. No answer. She called the police station and asked for the detective.

"I'm sorry, he can't come to the phone. I can take a message for him."

"That's okay. Never mind."

Tally was torn. Mrs. Gerg was calling out for her. She had to go and see what had happened. Had to make sure she was protected from Walter and Thet and his associate. Or Mateo and Raul? And maybe Ira? Well, not Raul, since he was in custody at the moment. She called Yolanda.

"I can't get hold of Jackson."

"Of course not. He's questioning Raul."

"But I really have to get to the hospital. I'm afraid Mrs. Gerg might be in danger." She had an idea. "Why don't you go to the police station yourself? Maybe someone will tell you something. Or they'll question him and release him. You could drive him home."

"Drive home a murderer?"

"Yolanda, do you believe that Raul murdered anyone?"

Tally heard her let out her breath. "No. Of course not. And that's a good idea. I'll go down there."

Tally let out a breath herself after she cut the call. She shifted into Drive and hurried as fast as she could without breaking too many traffic rules.

The nurse had left word at the front counter to let Tally up to Mrs. Gerg's room. She hoped they were being selective and weren't letting anyone else get to her. She was shocked at what she saw when she entered the room. Mrs. Gerg looked even smaller than she was. Her short curly hair was smashed flat on one side, her scalp shining through the thinness on top under the bright light over the head of her bed. She had an IV in one arm and machines displayed squiggles and emitted high-pitched beeps. She also had a wrapping on the other arm and bruises on one side of her face. The room smelled even more medicinal than the hallway had.

Tally stopped in the doorway, shocked by her frail appearance.

A woman in scrubs appeared beside Tally. "Are you Tally Holt? I'm the nurse who called you, Ann Davids."

Tally shook her extended hand. "What happened to her? When did she get here?"

The nurse went to Mrs. Gerg's bedside, examined her IV bag and started checking the readouts on the beeping machines. "A bad fall. She's been to X-ray and had some scans. There's no internal injury. We can be thankful for that. Mostly the fractured ulna and two phalanges."

Tally saw the brace on her forearm and the splints on two of her fingers then. Her injuries were all on her right side. She knew Mrs. Gerg was right-handed.

An announcement of a Code Blue came from the hallway.

"I'd better go see if I can help," the nurse said, and vanished.

Tally approached the bed. The head of Mrs. Gerg's bed was reeled up and a television on the wall ran with the volume low.

"What happened? Did someone do this to you?"

The poor woman smiled. "Like she said, a bad fall."

Tally could understand her now. Her voice was soft and slurred. Maybe she was on powerful painkillers. That would account for her speech. It didn't seem that her jaw was broken. "Where did you fall? In your house?"

She nodded. "Basement stairs."

Tally felt a chill creep up her spine. "Were you pushed?" She remembered how careful Mrs. Gerg always was on her steep basement stairs.

Mrs. Gerg looked at her full-on. "I don't know."

Tally knew, though.

"They're letting me go home tonight. I'm all fixed up."

"No. You can't go back there. Walter was trying to kill you."

"It wasn't Walter. He wasn't in the kitchen."

The door to her basement stairs was in the kitchen. "Where was he?"

"I'm not…sure." Her eyes tried to close.

"Who was in the kitchen?"

Mrs. Gerg grinned. "I was." She seemed awfully dopy. Could she have been pushed from behind and not realize it had happened?

"Were those other men in the house? Thet and Arlen?"

She studied the ceiling a moment. "Maybe Thet. Maybe Arlen. He's so tall. Don't remember. Three of them, I think." She frowned. "Or two."

Tally leaned close to her and spoke softly. "You can't go back home tonight. Come stay with me."

"Why on earth would I do that?"

Tally put a hand on the shoulder of her good arm, the one with the IV. "Just until we figure out exactly what happened. I don't want anything else bad to happen to you."

"Oh, don't worry. They'll take good care of me."

Tally took a seat in the one guest chair. She would wait until they discharged her, then take her home. At least there was no sign of any of the suspect men here. She wondered how Mrs. Gerg had gotten to the hospital. Had the men in the van brought her? Walter was still not walking. She wasn't sure whether he could walk or not, but he wasn't doing it very much.

"Ms. Holt?"

Tally jerked awake. The nurse stood in front of her, smiling. "You fell asleep."

She checked the bed. Mrs. Gerg was still there. "Do you know when she's being discharged?"

"We're ready right now. That's why I woke you. Do you know who is taking her home?"

"I am." Tally stood and gave Mrs. Gerg what she hoped was a look of reassurance.

"There are some papers you need to sign for us to release her in your care. Follow me."

Tally followed Nurse Davids down the hallway and around the corner to a station where she filled out what seemed like a lot of unnecessary forms. One of them looked useful: the release instructions. When she had signed the last one and gotten copies to take with her, she made her way back to the room.

Mrs. Gerg was gone.

20

Tally dashed back to the nurses' station where she'd signed the release papers.

"She's gone! Mrs. Gerg isn't there."

The nurse, Ann Davids, was still there doing paperwork. She looked up, a puzzled look wrinkling her brow, and followed Tally as she rushed back to the room.

"Did you see anyone in here?" she asked.

"I was going to ask you. I'm afraid maybe the man who pushed her down the stairs has her."

"Someone pushed her? That's not what she told us." The nurse stood still and turned, alarmed.

Tally started hyperventilating.

"Are you sure?" the nurse asked.

"Not positive," she said in between breaths. "But...what if he did?"

"She might still be here." The nurse checked Mrs. Gerg's bathroom, then left to check out some other places.

But Tally could see the IV needle dangling at the end of the tube. A large, empty plastic bag that had probably held her clothes lay on the bed, the hospital gown thrown there beside it.

Eventually, the nurse came back. Tally pointed out the clothing bag and the gown and the nurse agreed she was probably gone. "I called her but didn't get any answer. Can you check her home?" the nurse asked.

Tally said she would and drove to Mrs. Gerg's house.

* * * *

At the end of a long, hard day alone in the shop, Yolanda got a call from Raul asking her to pick him up at the police station. Since he had been taken there from the shop earlier in a police car, he didn't have any transportation with him. He had tried Lily, he said, but she wasn't answering. Yolanda hadn't gotten anywhere trying to see him or the detective earlier, so she had returned to work, then ended up closing her shop early. It had been such a difficult day. She couldn't have been more distracted.

"Sure, I can do that. I'll be there in a few minutes." She had been home for an hour, and had already eaten a light supper. She had been settling in to watch an old movie to take her mind off things. She had to admit she was relieved when Raul finally called. Eager to talk to him and learn more, she picked up her purse and car keys and headed for her front door, still on the phone.

"Thanks so much. I really appreciate it. You can drop Mateo at my place if you don't have time to take him home."

"Mateo?" She stopped at the door. Did she want to take him home? Did she want him in her car? "Raul, I have to do a couple of things first, then I'll be there. It won't take long. Hang on, okay?"

She called Tally. "I need a favor."

"When?"

"Well, right now."

"Yo, this is a bad time. I have to find Mrs. Gerg."

"She's missing? I thought you went to talk to her at the hospital."

"I did, but she disappeared. She's not here."

Yolanda retraced her steps and sat on her couch while Tally told her about the injuries and about the disappearance from the hospital. "One of Walter's friends probably got her," Yolanda said. "What can you do?"

After a moment of hesitating silence, Tally admitted she didn't know. "The nurse asked me to check her home, so that's where I'm headed now."

Yolanda tried to calculate how long that would take.

"What did you want from me?" Tally asked.

"Oh, man. This is such bad timing. Raul wants me to drive him and Mateo home from the police station and I'm kind of afraid of Mateo. I don't mind driving Raul, but he asked me to drop Mateo, too."

"Have either of them been charged with anything?"

Yolanda told her they'd both been picked up for questioning. "That's all I know. Raul didn't say anything about charges."

"At least they're not being held, right? They're letting them go."

"That doesn't mean they're not guilty. Does it? Does it?"

"Yolanda, calm down. I thought you trusted Raul."

"I do, but I don't trust Mateo and I don't think Raul does, either."

"You'll be okay with Raul there, though, won't you? Drop Mateo off first so you're not alone with him. Look, I'll see if Mrs. Gerg is home. I'm almost to her house. I'll call you back in a few minutes."

Yolanda started pacing, hoping for a call from Tally before she had to leave.

* * * *

The call renewed Tally's unease about Lily and Raul's budding relationship. She was getting whiplash from swinging her opinion of Raul, flailing right and left inside her head, over and over, up and down, every which way. She was glad Raul hadn't called Lily for the ride. She was younger and, maybe, more innocent, easily led. A small wave of guilt washed over her for thinking that it was perfectly all right for Yolanda, but not for Lily. But why hadn't he called Lily? Did he want to protect Lily from Mateo?

Tally was almost to her destination. She would help Yolanda out as soon as she could.

She slowed her car down coming up to Mrs. Gerg's house. The shiny white van with the blue sign crouched at the curb in front of her house. Those awful men must be there. She had no desire to see Thet or Arlen or Walter, but she had to find out where Mrs. Gerg was and if she was okay.

Squaring her shoulders and marching more confidently than she felt, she got to the front door and rang the doorbell. Her heart was doing double time and her finger shook a bit on the doorbell button.

Mrs. Gerg herself opened the door.

"Tally, what are you doing here?" She sounded chipper, like her old self.

Tally tried to see around her, to peer into the room. "Is someone here with you?"

"Yes, yes—see, I'm fine." She threw the door open and Tally saw all three men, sitting on her living room furniture, right at home, looking like they belonged there. A fourth man sat on the couch with them, a short, stout, dark man who looked like an older version of Thet Thura. Both men had darkish skin, brown eyes, and straight black hair, with similar noses and chins. Knowing that the jade came from Myanmar, she surmised both men were Burmese. They had to be involved in the smuggling. Didn't they?

"This is Mr. Thura's uncle, Mr. Win," said Mrs. Gerg, gesturing to the frowning man whose eyes were attempting to bore a hole through Tally's head. "Do you want to come in?" She swept her arm toward an upholstered chair that was perilously close to Mr. Win and the rest. It was also the chair Mrs. Gerg had probably been sitting in.

Mrs. Gerg swayed with her gesture so that Tally stepped forward to catch her if she fell. The splints on her fingers and the brace on her arm looked heavy. She had to feel lopsided.

Tally did want to come in, but she also needed to help Yolanda. "Maybe a little later? Could you just tell me one thing?"

Mrs. Gerg smiled her usual warm smile. Was she in danger? She didn't seem to think so.

"When you fell down the stairs, what happened? Who called the ambulance?"

"Why, I did. Aren't cell phones wonderful? No one else was here, so I just pulled it out of my pocket and called."

"Yes, they are wonderful. I'm glad you had it on you." What if she had lain on the floor of the basement for hours, injured? At least that didn't happen. She stepped as close to the older woman as she could and tried to talk so the men couldn't hear her. "Are you going to be all right here by yourself?"

The woman smiled again. "I'm not by myself. Yes, I'm fine. You run along if you have errands."

Tally was reluctant to leave, but what could she do? She couldn't force her way in and sit and stare at everyone just in case someone was going to do something bad.

She would check back later. When she got to her car, Tally called the hospital and left a message for the nurse, saying that Mrs. Gerg was home and seemed fine. She wasn't going to say she *was* fine. Tally wasn't quite sure that was true. She hoped it was, though. Surely, Mrs. Gerg would know if she had been pushed.

Next, she called Yolanda. After a moment of discussion they decided that, instead of the two of them being together in a car, Tally would merely tail Yolanda while she dropped the two cousins at their respective homes, Mateo first.

Tally and Yolanda met at Yolanda's after that was done.

"What happened at the station?" Tally asked, taking a sip of the iced tea Yolanda had poured her. They stood in Yolanda's kitchen, both leaning against the counters. "Did Raul tell you?"

"He said they asked him the same questions over and over."

"Yeah, that's what they do," Tally said. "They have to see if the story changes or not."

"He said he didn't have any answers to their questions, except the ones about where he'd been on certain days. They wanted to know if he'd seen some specific items and if he'd taken them. Stolen them. They showed him pictures of watches and jewelry, and some old coins. Even a few framed paintings."

"Did they say anything about the jade stones?"

"I don't know. Raul didn't mention that."

"What did Mateo say?"

"He didn't. No one said anything until after I dropped him off. Then Raul wanted to tell me everything that happened at the station."

Tally frowned. "Wouldn't he want to know how Mateo's questioning went?"

Yolanda shrugged. "Maybe they talked about it before I got there. It was tense between them, I thought. Raul sat in front and directed Mateo to the back seat. Maybe Raul is mad at Mateo for getting him mixed up in all this."

"Do you still think Raul stole anything?"

"No, I really never did. I just...wasn't sure."

After finishing the tea, Tally wended her way home, thinking about the thefts, the jade, Mrs. Gerg, those four awful men at her house, and the Crime Fritzers. And the murder of the man on crutches, Sawyer Sutton. Oh yes, and the jewelry Ira had probably stolen and given to Dorella. Did he steal it? Or were Walter, or those other men, a part of the crime ring? They had had a pile of jewelry and it was now gone from Mrs. Gerg's house. Nothing made sense. She called Jackson and got his voice mail, but didn't leave a message.

Nigel greeted her at the door, starving nearly to death, if his shrill noises were any indication.

"You poor baby," she crooned, hefting him into her arms and carrying him to the kitchen and saving him from an almost certain imminent death from malnourishment and, ultimately, starvation. He graced her with a thankful glance before digging in and making short work of his din-din.

Her phone rang before she could sit down and relax. It was her mother again.

"Hi Mom. How's Rome going now?" Now that they were out of jail and not accused of smuggling powdered sugar anymore.

Her mother was panting and took a moment to catch her breath before she could speak. "It's flooding here. It's a huge disaster. We have to leave. But I don't know if we can."

Flooding? Now what? "Another disaster? Have you done any shows there yet?"

Her dad's voice came on the line. "It's no good here, Tally. There's so much water. Everything is flooded and we can't get anywhere."

"Where are you?"

"We almost made it to the airport, then the cab had to stop. The roads were all closed. We're in a small second-floor restaurant that's full of people. Everyone is trying to leave and they closed the venue down."

The Circus Maximus. "It's been there for centuries. Will it be okay?"

"I'm sure it will, eventually, but no one can get anywhere. There's no point in doing a performance here. No one would be able to come see us. I've been on the phone with the travel agent we usually use."

Tally was getting worried about them. Lately, they stumbled upon disasters everywhere they went. "Can you go to another continent? Africa? Australia?" Surely there was somewhere they could perform in the whole wide world. Somewhere that wasn't flooding and that airplanes were flying to.

"We're working on it. It's kind of a mess here. I was able to get two tickets to Japan, but the flight took off before we could get to the airport."

"Dad, it's not safe where you are. You and Mom need to get somewhere safe."

"Japan will be safe." His words sounded assured, but his voice was strained.

"But you can't get there. Where can you get to? Take the next flight, wherever it goes. Well, maybe not if it goes back to Gibraltar. You might get stuck there again."

She got a small chuckle out of her father. "We'll let you know, sweetheart."

After the call ended, she thumbed through her phone to find news from Italy and found that not only was Rome flooding, but many other cities had the same problem, especially Venice, which was half underwater to start with. They had had record amounts of rain all over the whole country. Her parents sure could pick places to go that were having disasters. They should have been reporters, covering sensational stories around the globe. All they would have to do is book a flight and a disaster would be waiting for them when they arrived. If they could get there.

21

On Wednesday morning, Raul got a phone call at work. Yolanda saw the look of gaping alarm on his face. She started toward him to find out what was the matter, but he backed away.

"Be back in a minute," he said, and stepped out the back door.

Puzzled, she peered out the window. Raul was distressed. He was normally a calm, undemonstrative person. Not right now, though. He shook his head, then his fist, grimaced, and spoke forcefully into the phone. It looked like his voice was probably raised, but wasn't loud enough for Yolanda to hear. *It must be Mateo*, she surmised. New developments?

When Raul closed the call, he stared down the alley, standing perfectly still for a few seconds. Yolanda scurried back to the middle of the shop so he wouldn't know she had spied on him. He entered the back room with an angry scowl on his face.

"Stupid Mateo," he spat, tossing his phone onto the countertop with a clatter.

"Don't break it," Yolanda said, catching the phone before it slid onto the floor. She waited for him to spill. She knew he would.

He gave an exasperated sigh and turned his sad eyes on her. Sad was better than angry, she thought.

"They came to his apartment early this morning. He was still in bed and he let them in."

"Who's *they*?"

"The cops. They had a search warrant."

"Then he had to let them in, no?"

"I guess so. Couldn't he have called a lawyer?"

Yolanda doubted that either Mateo or Raul knew any lawyers they could call. "That might not help. What happened?"

"They found some stuff. They arrested him."

"Whoa, sit down. Tell me." She pulled out the chair to her desk and practically pushed him into it. "What did they find?"

He looked like he might cry. "He had some of the stolen stuff." Raul's voice shook. "The things they showed us pictures of yesterday. He had those. Some of those."

"He's part of the local theft ring? He's been breaking into houses in Fredericksburg?"

He shook his head. "I could have sworn he didn't do that."

"But he has the stolen items."

"Just a few of them, he said. Two pieces of jewelry, a ring and a pair of earrings. He told me he didn't steal them. But—this is the stupid part—he wanted to. He wanted to get in with the Crime Fritzers, the ones who were robbing houses, but they wouldn't let him in. That's what he told me, over and over. *Muy stupido*." Raul banged his fist on the wooden desktop.

"Are all of the Crime Fritzers doing this?"

"No, no. Just a few. I bet most of them don't know a thing about it."

"What did he have? Where did he get it?" Yolanda was trying to make sense of this. Mateo wanted to steal things, but the ones in the ring wouldn't let him join them? And now he had the stolen goods? "Did he lie to y'all?"

"He never has lied to me before. He doesn't always tell me everything he does. He knows I wouldn't approve of some of it, but I don't know. I don't know if he's lying now or not."

Yolanda thought it was obvious his cousin was lying, but she didn't want to say that to Raul. "I don't understand what you're saying."

"He told me that Ira gave him those things. Mateo has been dating a new girl—I met her once and she's nice— and Ira said he should give her the earrings and ring, but the ring didn't fit her and she didn't like the earrings."

"Ira? Ira Mann?"

"He has a lot more money than Mateo."

"So, Mateo only had those things because his new girlfriend doesn't like them. How many other things has he given her that she did like?"

Raul shook his head. "He's an idiot."

"Raul, maybe Ira stole the things. Maybe Mateo didn't do it."

"I told him to tell the cops about Ira, but he said he won't. He doesn't want to be a rat, he said. So stupid."

"You could tell them. Or we could, together."

"He said he might later, but doesn't want to yet. Please don't say anything, okay? He might tell them on his own."

Of course she wouldn't, if Raul didn't want her to. But she would try to make him want her to. It didn't make sense for Mateo to be accused of Ira's crimes. If Mateo was telling his cousin the truth. She was sure Raul would do the right thing. He always did.

The phone rang and Yolanda answered to find someone wanting a special order. Forty tiny baskets to use at place settings for a small wedding reception. It was a challenging concept. Both she and Raul dove into it, tossing ideas back and forth and getting excited about the job. Tiny pieces of wedding veil looped on the basket handles, pastel mints, baby's breath, silk linings in blue and green, the bride's colors. They both pushed Mateo to the backs of their minds.

* * * *

Lily was distracted. She dropped a cup of sugar on the kitchen floor and nearly burst into tears. Tally wanted to talk to her about Raul, to see if that's what was troubling her, but it felt like Lily was closing herself off, putting up a wall. She didn't look at Tally all morning, didn't speak directly to her, even when she first arrived. She usually greeted Tally with a cheerful "good morning," but today she had come in, tied on her apron, and set to work with a grim look on her face.

Tally kept her distance. She hoped Lily knew she was available to talk to, when she got to that point. They worked side by side with Molly and, when she got there, Dorella.

One bright spot happened midmorning.

"My dad has an interview, Ms. Holt," Molly said, trying to sound offhand about her statement, letting a tiny bit of excitement come through.

"That's wonderful," Tally said. "At the junior college?"

"Yes. He applied and they said his paperwork looks good. They want to talk to him sometime soon."

"They didn't set up a date and time?"

"Well, no. Dad said he had to look at Mom's chemo schedule."

Tally nodded, hoping this would work out.

In the afternoon, Tally was in her office going over her payroll records. Payday was coming up and she liked to be on top of things a couple of days early.

She was interrupted by another call from her mother's number. She snatched her cell from the desk and opened the call.

"Mom? Dad? Where are you? Are you okay?"

Her dad answered. "We are, finally." She could hear the relief in his voice. He sounded so much more relaxed than the last call, when they were trying to get to the airport through the floods in Rome. "We made it to Sydney."

They had taken her advice and gone to a new continent. She smiled at the thought. Australia sounded like a calm, safe place. It wasn't in the news at the moment, anyway. "Australia! That was a long flight. Any disasters there?"

"Not yet." She could hear the smile in his voice. "We didn't do our shows in Japan, since we couldn't get there, and had to cancel in Rome. But it looks like smooth sailing here."

"How's Mom?"

"She saw a doctor for her throat. The damp from the flooding really got to her. She has some cough syrup that is some kind of miracle stuff, I think. She's on the mend."

"Are you doing any shows there?"

"We're booked for the weekend. Friday, Saturday, and Sunday. A local theater had a group cancel and we were able to step in and fill their slot."

Tally felt the weight lift that had been on the portion of her mind reserved for worry about her parents. "That's so good, Dad. That's great. Tell Mom to take it easy."

"She'll be fine. You know her."

She did. She knew both of them. The show must go on.

Doing her sisterly duty, she called Cole to relay the news on their parents.

"I'm on my way."

"What? There's no emergency here," she said.

"My installation is finished. I got paid and I'm all done here. I'm coming to see you."

"Me? And Nigel?"

"Nigel? Oh, the cat. Sure."

"And…"

He chuckled. "You got me. Yes, I'd like to see Dorella."

She glanced at the time as she closed the call. It was nearly time for her to close up. She wanted to get the payroll done before she left, so she went back to it, but only for five minutes. Then her cell rang again and she almost ignored it, being in the middle of FICA calculations. A glance showed her Mrs. Gerg's number, though, so she answered it in case the poor woman was having more trouble.

"Tally? I'm so glad I caught you." She sounded breathless.

"Are you all right? Have you been running?"

"Not really. No. Just…could you come over here?" Her voice was breaking. She was in distress, Tally thought.

"Where are you? At home?"

"It would be good if you…yes, if you hurried over right away. Without stopping for anything."

Tally frowned. That was an odd request. "What would I stop for?"

"Can you just do it?" The older woman's voice rose with each word, higher and thinner.

"Don't get upset, Mrs. Gerg. Sure, I can come over."

"Right away?" Now she sounded on the verge of tears.

"Yes, I'm leaving right this minute." Tally stood and thought for a moment. Something was wrong. This wasn't like Mrs. Gerg at all. She was sure it had to do with those awful men. She called Jackson Rogers, but he didn't answer. Not trusting her message to voice mail, she called the station and left word there that she thought Mrs. Gerg might need assistance and to send someone there. On her way out, she also told Dorella, who was in the kitchen, where she was going.

"Would you please call Jackson Rogers in a few minutes and see if you can get him? Ask him to go to Mrs. Gerg's. I have a bad feeling about this." She wrote his number on one of the cards they stuck in with the orders. "I probably won't be back to close up, but I can come over later. I need to finish my work in the office tonight anyway." She yelled thanks to her workers as she went out the back door.

As soon as she got into the car, she also called Yolanda. She didn't answer, either, but Tally left a message this time.

"Yo, something is wrong at Mrs. Gerg's. Very wrong. I just spoke to her and I have a terrible feeling. I'm going over there. I don't trust that Walter Wright fellow, or his buddies. I can't get Jackson on the phone. Could you try to call and tell him? And ask him to come over there to check it out?"

She didn't want to be there alone.

22

Yolanda was alarmed when she finally listened to the message. Tally had sounded frightened. She shouldn't be going to that place. She should have waited. Yolanda tried to call Detective Rogers at the station, but they just said they would give him a message.

"Raul, go ahead and order the things we talked about. I need to run out for a minute."

First, she would go to the station to find Detective Jackson Rogers. Then, although it frightened her to think about it, she would go to Mrs. Gerg's to give Tally support. Or backup. Or whatever she might need. She didn't have a choice.

* * * *

There were no cars in front of Mrs. Gerg's house when Tally pulled up to the curb. Had the men left? She didn't know why she did it, but she got out of her car quietly and shut the door without slamming it. The dead quiet on the block was eerie. She made no noise getting onto the porch and up to the front door, then stood still, listening for a half a minute or so. The drapes at the front of the house were all drawn, which wasn't usual for Mrs. Gerg. The door didn't have any glass, or any way to see inside. The dark porch didn't offer any clues. She tried the knob, but it was locked.

Finally, she rang the bell, fervently hoping the woman was alone in the house.

Mrs. Gerg came to the door and opened it a few inches with her left hand. Tally could see that she still wore the brace on her arm and the splints on her two broken fingers.

"Tally? Is that you?"

Tally stared at her. "You can see me, can't you? Yes, it's me." What was going on? Was she trying to tell her something? Did she need Tally to help her?

"I mean, just you?"

Tally took a step back, her nape prickling, her stomach feeling leaden. She should not go into that house.

In a flash, the door was flung open and Arlen grasped her wrists with an iron grip and yanked her inside, slamming the door. Walter stood just inside, looking completely able-bodied. He turned the lock in the door. There was no boot on his foot and Tally didn't see any crutches anywhere. Had he been faking his injury? Or maybe just extending his recovery period? The older man, Thet Thura's uncle, was on the couch next to his nephew, doing nothing. Tally felt the older man was participating, though. He watched so carefully, she thought he might be in charge of everything they were doing. Arlen glanced at him as he held Tally.

Tally tried to pull herself away from the odious man. His breath stunk of tobacco. She managed the beginnings of a scream before Thet jumped up and he and Arlen overpowered her, in a flash taping her mouth and securing her wrists behind her with thick swatches of duct tape, ripped noisily off a large roll.

Mrs. Gerg had stood frozen, watching them tie up Tally. Now it was her turn, to Tally's horror. They grabbed both her arms and taped them together behind her. Mrs. Gerg gave a huge flinch when Walter gripped her where the brace held her broken arm together.

"Now, both of you, downstairs," Arlen said, snarling.

Tally tried to trip him, but he nimbly avoided her outstretched foot. Arlen shook her roughly from behind and propelled her toward the door in the kitchen that led to the steep basement stairs, the ones Mrs. Gerg said she had fallen down.

Were they going to throw her down the stairs to the concrete floor? Were they going to throw both of them down there?

Tally stopped struggling on her way down so she wouldn't fall to the hard cement. She didn't want to land with one or two of the men on top of her. Without her hands to break a fall, she might even crack her head at the bottom.

Thet manhandled Mrs. Gerg behind her and soon all four were in the basement. There was no sign of the man who was Thet's countryman and uncle. Walter had followed them. Now he strode, on perfectly good legs, to an old, battered wooden door and threw it open.

"In here," Walter said to Arlen, nodding sharply to the inside of the dark room beyond the small door.

"What? You're just gonna leave them here?" Thet answered.

"For now. We'll do something more permanent just before we leave. We're not ready to leave yet."

Both women were thrown to the floor and the door was shut. Tally heard a key being turned in the lock.

The darkness in the room was flat and black at first, but there was a dull light source, a small, high window. It was nighttime outside, but some gray light made its way in eventually, as her eyes adjusted.

Tally could tell that Mrs. Gerg lay beside her. Not daring to make a sound, Tally scooted to her and held her ear to the woman's nose. She was breathing. Had her head collided with the floor when she was pushed down? There was no blood. Mrs. Gerg's mouth was taped, too. Walter must have done that behind her upstairs. She hadn't seen it happening. Tiny sobs escaped from behind the tape over Mrs. Gerg's mouth. Her broken bones were probably throbbing after that brutal treatment.

One benefit of the rough handling had been that Tally's wrist bonds were loosened. She managed to sit up in the dim room and began to work at them.

* * * *

Yolanda started toward Mrs. Gerg's house, feeling it was urgent that she get there. She had only gone two blocks when her phone rang. It was her father. She knew he would keep calling if she ignored him, so she resigned herself, pulled over to concentrate, and answered it.

"Papa? How are you tonight?"

"I am upset. I am furious. Can you guess why?"

Yolanda squeezed her eyes shut and gritted her teeth to keep from screaming. In the most pleasant voice she could manage, she answered. "No, Papa. I cannot guess why. What's the matter?"

"You know what is the matter." If he had been in front of her, she was fairly certain she would have gotten wet from his spit. Violetta. It must be about her. She was the only person he invested that amount of emotion in. "I have talked to our priest. Now do you know why I am angry?"

"I'm sorry. You'll have to tell me. I don't have much time, so tell me quickly, please." Her own anger level was rising. If he didn't quit playing his guessing game, she would reach his own level soon.

"You knew all about Violetta and Eden, didn't you?"

"Papa, all y'all knew, too. You and Mom. She told you. Just before y'all disowned her and kicked her out." Yolanda's words were not kind. It was not a kind thing he had done to his beloved daughter.

"But this is going too far. It's an abomination. Our priest told me what they are intending to do. Vi talked to him about it. Not only is our family disgraced, they are disgracing the sacrament of marriage, pretending they can have a wedding. Get married. No priest should perform a ceremony like that. I hope they are not going through with this. You will talk to them. They cannot do this."

"Papa, there are plenty of clergy who will marry them. They *are* getting married. My turn now. Can y'all guess why no one told you?"

She screamed her last words and cut off the call. The man was impossible. But now he knew for sure that they were getting married. He wouldn't feel completely disgraced, maybe, since they were doing it in Dallas, where no one knew their family. Her angry words seemed to echo in her car.

She nearly screamed again when her phone rang in her hand before she could set it down. She had pulled into traffic and knew she wasn't supposed to be on her phone while driving, so she let it go and proceeded to East College Street, Mrs. Gerg's street. She turned toward where she thought her house was.

Yolanda drove down the street, slowly, not sure which house was Mrs. Gerg's. She knew she was on the right block, though. Tally's car wasn't there. That was a relief. She hadn't come here alone. She'd been afraid she would do that. Yolanda tried to call her, but no one answered. Stopping in the middle of the block, she pondered her options. First, she could go to the door and talk to Mrs. Gerg once she figured out which house it was. *If* she could figure out which one it was. Second, she could leave and see if Tally was home or at her shop. Third, she could try the detective once more.

She decided on number three and picked up the phone to call him but noticed that the call she hadn't answered while driving was from her sister. No doubt her father had called and harassed her. She needed to call Vi in case she was awfully upset by their insensitive, intolerant father.

"Vi, are you okay?" she said when Vi answered immediately.

"I am. But remind me again why I tell you anything."

She shouldn't have talked to their father about the wedding at all. If she could have kicked herself, seated in her car, she would have. The way she remembered it was that Vi didn't care if she told him, but that Vi herself wasn't going to.

"The priest told him. I just verified it. He was going to find out eventually. Don't you think he has to know?"

"I told you that. No. He never needs to know. I never need to talk to him again."

Yolanda composed herself for a second. "I see that I shouldn't have talked to him. I won't do that again. You and he can handle your relationship. I'll keep out of it."

Vi gave a bitter laugh. "Relationship. There is no relationship. I've disowned him."

"Are you...disowning me, too?"

This laugh was gentle. "Never, sister. I'll never disown you. I love you. But please do stay out from between us, okay?"

Yolanda finished the call, relieved that Vi wasn't as angry with her at the end of it. Then she dialed Jackson Rogers, hoping that he would answer this time.

* * * *

Tally didn't have a way to tell time in the dark cellar. Her cell phone was in her purse, which, the last time she saw it, was on the floor just inside Mrs. Gerg's front door, where she'd dropped it when she was grabbed.

She was worried about Mrs. Gerg. She hadn't moved in a while. Tally was relieved when the woman finally gave a groan, muffled by the duct tape, and started moving her legs. Tally puffed out a sigh of relief that the woman was reviving. Mrs. Gerg seemed to be trying to sit up. Tally couldn't help her with her own hands bound behind her. They sought each other's eyes through the murkiness and wordlessly gave each other encouragement. It wouldn't do to make noise and have the men come down to the basement. Tally had already been working at her own loosened bonds for what seemed like a long time and she renewed her efforts, feeling a tiny amount of give, bit by bit.

They were in a dank-smelling room, not very large. The walls seemed blackened. Tally looked around and glanced up at the small, high window, the only source of light—dim, nighttime light. Trying to squirm closer to Mrs. Gerg, she realized she was disturbing a layer of black dust on the floor. Coal. This room had to have been a coal bin back when people had coal furnaces in Fredericksburg. If she could get free, she might be able to get out through that window. The ceiling was low, so the window wouldn't be that high when she stood up. If she ever got that far. She knew she could fit through it. She would have to.

She could hear the men upstairs perfectly. The sound between the main floor and the basement carried well. She would have to stay quiet. Walter and Thet were talking in hushed voices, probably in the kitchen. Arlen's boots thumped back and forth somewhere, like he was pacing. She didn't hear any other voices.

The peal of the doorbell cut through the whispers and the silence. A chair scraped on the wooden floor above and footsteps crossed the kitchen, toward the front door. Did the older man ever speak? She didn't remember hearing his voice.

Tally doubled, tripled her efforts to free her hands. Bending her fingers and scratching at the tape with her nails.

She heard the door open. Two pair of footsteps came into the kitchen. They were followed by a third, Arlen's, Tally thought, by the clomping of his cowboy boots.

"Do you know where they went?" A familiar voice! That was Jackson! He was here, looking for her!

She pounded her feet on the cement floor a few times, to no avail. It didn't make any sound and it hurt her heels. She wrenched her shoulders and squirmed, pulling at the tape. She had to scream and let him know they were down here. She tried to lower her hands and bring them in front of her so she could rip the tape off her mouth. The bonds were still too tight.

Walter answered Jackson. "They went shopping. Candy needed some groceries and Ms. Holt took her."

"Here's my card. Call me as soon as they get back." Tally heard Jackson's footsteps in his sturdy shoes heading for the front door.

Her desperate screams were tiny, muted squeaks that carried about halfway to the stairs.

The front door opened and closed and one man came back to the kitchen.

"You were right," Thet said. "It's a good thing we moved both the cars."

A third, deeper voice joined in. "This was never a good plan, Thet." Though she had never heard his voice, she knew that was the uncle. Win. He gave her the creeps even more than Thet and Arlen did.

Tally quit struggling and grew still so she could listen. What plan were they talking about? The plan to kill her and Mrs. Gerg?

The deep voice went on. "If you and your idiot cousins hadn't put the goods into the wrong shipment, we would have gotten it, sold it, and be back home by now."

"We realized it right away, though, Uncle Win." Thet sounded subservient, a high, wheedling tone in his voice. Trying to convince his uncle? Groveling? "We tried to get the shipment derailed so it wouldn't get to the shop here in Fredericksburg. I hired two men to intercept everything, carry out a fake hijacking, and get the goods to me. We couldn't have predicted the hijacking would go wrong and the shipment would actually get to the wrong destination."

Tally would have gasped if her mouth hadn't been covered in duct tape. He arranged the hijacking. He had to be the person who somehow contacted Mateo and Sutton, too. And hired them to steal his smuggled stones off the truck. How crazy, Tally thought.

"Or that the pieces would melt and expose the jade, Uncle Win. If Mateo and Sawyer had pulled off the fake hijacking, the jade would be in Dallas right now, in the aquarium shop, where it's supposed to be."

"I didn't travel all the way to Texas to cry over what went wrong." Tally shivered at the sound of that deep, cold, accusing tone. "I'm here to make things right. Now we just have to clean up."

Clean up? Tally didn't like the sound of that.

Walter's voice joined them. "How are you going to do that, Mr. Win?"

"We have most of the jade back," the older man said, his voice softening a bit. "You did good, Thet, and you too, Arlen, finding out where it was and eliminating that threat."

"Sawyer, you mean," Walter said. "Sawyer Sutton. I think I'm the one who figured out he had it."

"You did," Thet said. "That was good." It sounded like he was talking to a small child. Tally wondered if he was patting him on the head. She thought Walter might be out of his depth with these men. In over his head.

The older man went on. "Anyway, he's gone, Sawyer. Who else do we need to take care of?"

"Besides those two in the basement?" Arlen asked.

Tally's hopes died. *Clean up. Take care of.* They intended to kill the two of them. Her and poor Mrs. Gerg.

Mrs. Gerg had heard everything, too. Her frightened eyes stared upward, at the kitchen. Tally sagged and lay on the floor, hot tears falling into the coal dust beneath her.

23

Yolanda saw Jackson's car pull into the police station parking lot, where she was waiting for him in her own car. She shot out of the driver's seat and waved her arms to hail him. "Detective! Over here!"

He walked toward her. "Do you know where Tally is?" He looked worried.

"She told me she was going to Mrs. Gerg's, but I drove there and didn't see her car."

"Did you go to the door?"

She shook her head. "I wasn't sure which house it was. Tally was afraid for Mrs. Gerg's safety. I was afraid for Tally. I thought she might rush in there. So I didn't want to rush in, either."

"That's just as well. I think you should stay away from them. We're about to make a move on them."

"What for, exactly?" There were so many crimes going around lately, it was hard to keep track.

"I can't tell you everything that's going on. I shouldn't even be telling you this, but we have a person of interest in custody, regarding the murder at the motel, who has given us some good information. There are a few details to track down, but I don't want you near that place when we go after them."

"But what if Tally's there?"

He frowned. She could tell he wasn't sure if she was or not. Yolanda wished she knew where Tally was.

"They could have put her car somewhere else, right?" she said. "Maybe they've kidnapped her. Maybe she's injured." Yolanda realized she was waving her arms and put them down at her side. "I drove around town, to the grocery store and the drugstore she uses, and she's not there."

"Just you stay away, you hear? Let us handle it."

Yolanda nodded. It didn't look like they were going to make their move very soon, though. What if they "made a move" too late? She would talk to Raul one more time, then try to check Mrs. Gerg's neighborhood again, just a quick trip. She felt she was close to figuring some of this out. She wondered who was in custody and hoped that person could tell them what was going on. Mateo? Ira?

* * * *

Tally wriggled and squirmed, feeling she was close to getting the tape off her left hand. It was exhausting work, though. She took a break from struggling with her restraints and looked around the basement, her eyes now much better adjusted to the dark. The voices in the kitchen above had grown silent. The men had either gone out or were in another part of the house. If they had the jade, was it still here? At Mrs. Gerg's?

She stopped struggling to think. She stared at the floor. And then she saw something. The leaden-colored dust showed footprints leading to one of the corners of the room. The prints looked like they belonged to a large shoe, for a man's foot. On closer inspection, she saw the heel and the pointy toe of a cowboy boot. She followed the prints, scooting alongside them, being careful not to disturb the dust that held them. From the dusty markings, it looked like something had been set on the floor, maybe some boxes. Three of them were still there, shoebox- size. Had the men hidden something here? She peered into the corner, hoping to see a piece of jade. She didn't see one, but did see a tiny scrap of brown plastic. Was it her imagination, or did it look like it was from one of the failed replicas? Maybe a piece of fudge or Mary Jane?

What did that mean? The piece of the fake candy could mean that they had put the jade-filled plastic here temporarily. It obviously wasn't here any longer. One of them had to be responsible for the death of Sawyer Sutton, the guy with the broken leg. Mateo had crashed the delivery truck into Sutton's pickup when he had fallen asleep. Yolanda thought they had been meant to rendezvous. She had been right. For Sutton to steal the plastic. To divert the plastic from the destination of Bella's Baskets, because it wasn't supposed to be in that shipment. And when that didn't happen and it arrived at the basket shop, Sutton stole it from Yolanda's window. He was probably supposed to get it for the guys upstairs, Thet, Arlen, and Mr. Win. He must have decided to keep it himself. Maybe he didn't know what he'd been hired to do until he saw the melting plastic.

It sounded like these guys then killed him and took the jade back from him, planning to get it to an aquarium in Dallas where they could sell it. Fence it? An aquarium? A front for a smuggling operation? *It must be*, she reasoned.

Mrs. Gerg made a sound and Tally looked over at her. The woman jerked her head back, summoning Tally closer. So Tally scooted through the black dust again. She would never wear these jeans again. Mrs. Gerg threw her head in a circle and, finally, understanding dawned on Tally. She scrunched her back next to Mrs. Gerg's back and clawed at the other woman's bonds.

Maybe because the older woman's skin was drier, or maybe because her skin was old and loose, or maybe because of the splints on her fingers, her tape wasn't as tight as Tally's. In fact, she was able to find the end of it and tug on it, pulling it off entirely. Mrs. Gerg had both hands free!

The woman peeled the tape off her mouth, left-handed, with a painful ripping sound and took a couple of deep breaths before starting on Tally's bonds. It was awkward for her to maneuver around the two splinted fingers, but Mrs. Gerg would not give up. When they were both finally free, they stood and stretched their cramped and aching muscles in complete silence. Mrs. Gerg's finger dressings were no longer gleaming white. They were all in place, though. The arm brace had been tan to begin with, but it looked gray and dingy. Tally's eyes had adjusted well to the low light by now. They both kept their lips pressed together tight. It would be a disaster if the men upstairs heard them, came downstairs, and bound them again. It would no doubt be more securely this time.

Tally stepped cautiously to the place under the stairs where the scrap of plastic lay. When she picked it up, that was, indeed, exactly what it was. Her head whirred. The jade was definitely stored here at one point. She tried to peek inside the boxes. It was dark. She couldn't tell what was inside them. When she felt inside, she didn't feel plastic or stones. Maybe these were things Mrs. Gerg stored here.

Once more, Tally laid things out in her mind from everything that she'd overheard. At last, all the parts fit together to make the whole. The pieces of the puzzle fell together. They blended, like the ingredients of a complicated, sinister recipe.

From the factory, where it was illegally stuffed with Blood Jade, the plastic had been shipped overseas to the warehouse outside town, but addressed to an unintended destination instead of the smuggling headquarters, some aquarium shop in Dallas belonging to Arlen, maybe managed by Thet Thura. At the warehouse, the shipment was loaded onto the delivery truck driven by Mateo and bound for Yolanda's shop. Sutton was supposed to "hijack" the shipment so it could be given to Thet and sent, or taken, to Dallas. Was Mateo in on that? The plan fell apart when Mateo fell asleep at the wheel and caused the accident that left Sawyer Sutton with a broken leg. Mateo, who also wanted in on the crime watch theft ring, and maybe was part of this scheme, too, had been waylaid while another driver was sent to get the order to Bella's Baskets that same night. The warehouse manager was too diligent for the smugglers.

After that, the product lay in the window at Bella's Baskets, melting in the hot sun, starting to reveal the concealed contraband, when Sawyer Sutton limped past. That night, or early morning, the window was broken and Walter Wright was badly beaten there. Someone had made away with the pieces of jade and their containers, but that someone was not Walter Wright. From what Tally had seen upstairs recently, Walter—and Thet?—were part of the ring that broke into the houses they were supposed to be guarding and robbed them. It wasn't a stretch for Walter to break the window to try to steal the jade. But it didn't seem he had succeeded. Whoever beat him up probably had.

Since Walter had been beaten with a crutch, a detail he probably should not have let slip, Sawyer Sutton logically had the contraband at that point. He had been the person hired to waylay them for Thet and Win. The stones were supposed to go to Arlen's Dallas store from there, but didn't make it. So Sutton broke the window and took the plastic, and the jade, for himself, and checked into the cheap motel at the edge of town. Hiding there?

Then Sawyer, who hadn't hidden well enough, was killed and, it was again assumed, the jade taken from him. Strangled, according to what Jackson let slip accidently. Did his killer come here, to Mrs. Gerg's basement, from the murder scene? One of them killed Sawyer. Which one? Walter had been faking it, pretending his leg injury was worse than it was, but he *had* been injured. Tally didn't think he could have killed Sutton. His leg was genuinely too bad at that time. Thet seemed to be saying that he killed Sutton and Tally believed him.

Police hadn't found any stolen goods here when they searched Mrs. Gerg's house. Meanwhile, Yolanda had remembered she put some of the pieces in her shop, in a cupboard. The pieces they hadn't put into the window yet. Who else knew they were there?

Then, Dorella's boyfriend, Ira Mann, had been caught with goods stolen from houses while he made crime watch rounds, so he was part of the housebreaking ring. Which was maybe not the same group of thieves doing the smuggling.

Mateo may or may not have been a part of the crime watch ring, but he had some of the stolen goods. Given to him by Ira, he said. Maybe. Maybe not.

Why was Jackson here just now? Did he get another tip? He hadn't searched the house. Was he looking for her? Had Dorella called him as she'd asked? Was he searching for the stolen household items? Or for the jade?

She couldn't put all the pieces together from here. About the only thing she could do from here was wait for these men to murder her and Mrs. Gerg. She had to get out of this cold, dark cellar.

24

Yolanda had just parked two blocks from what she thought was Mrs. Gerg's house when Raul called her. Since Mateo was in custody, he wanted to get everything off his chest and she was the lucky recipient. She listened intently while he spilled out everything he knew from Mateo. He was breathless by the time he finished. And Yolanda was fuming.

She got out and slammed her car door extra-hard in her anger. What was Raul thinking? She was glad he decided he had to confess to someone, anyway, and glad that the someone was her. At least he wasn't the one Detective Rogers had in custody. But the information was late. She wished she had known all of this information much earlier.

Mateo was a wannabe in the crime watch ring, but he was a full participant in the much more serious crime, the smuggling of what he called Blood Jade. It was mined in Myanmar by impoverished people to enrich a few already wealthy, exploitative ones, much as blood diamonds were in Africa. He was deep into that, while he made everyone, including the police, believe he was on the edges. He was ignorant of what was going on for most of the time, of what was being smuggled, but went along with what he was told, like he usually did.

He had messed up the fake hijacking by falling asleep at the wheel and Sutton was left with a broken leg. And eventually, someone had found out where the treasure was and killed Sutton. Mateo didn't know who. How had they ever expected to double-cross international criminals?

When Mateo delivered the pizza to Sutton and found him dead, he hadn't even known where Sutton was staying or who that pizza was going to. Sutton hadn't even known Mateo was working that job. It was completely a coincidence. But not one the authorities were likely to believe.

What a mess! Yolanda had to tell all of this to the police. But first, she had to find out where Tally was.

Yolanda started to head for Mrs. Gerg's block on foot. Tally wasn't anywhere else. She must be there, Yolanda reasoned. She would do a careful search for her friend's car before the police got there. Maybe she could give them some information that might help locate Tally.

She turned around, after having thought this out. She would take her car rather than approach on foot. If she found Tally, they might have to get away quickly. Tally's car probably didn't have the keys inside if it had been moved and hidden.

* * * *

Mrs. Gerg was stronger than Tally thought. She bent over to let Tally climb onto her back, then onto her shoulders so Tally could reach the window. Tally put her palms flat on the cool cement wall to help her to balance. It didn't make her a lighter burden for Mrs. Gerg, but at least she didn't topple off of her back onto the hard floor. She reached up with one hand. She could feel the older woman's body trembling beneath her feet while she fumbled with the latch, managing to open the window. It only made a slight creaking noise. Tally wondered how many years it had been since it had been opened.

Clawing a grip on the lower sash with both hands, Tally pulled herself up until she was sprawling across the edge of the window on her stomach. She scrambled the rest of the way out and lay for a few seconds, composing herself. Her heart pounding. Her ears pulsing in time to her heartbeat. She looked back through the window. How had she done that? Lots of adrenaline, was her guess.

Now what? Should she try to haul Mrs. Gerg out, too? She poked her head back through the opening and whispered, "Give me your hand. I'll try to pull you out."

Mrs. Gerg shook her head violently. "No," she whispered back. "You go ahead. You can't lift me."

Tally thought she was probably right. The woman only had full use of one hand. It was unlikely she would be able to hoist herself out, even with Tally pulling her up. If she *could* pull her up. That would take another mighty adrenaline burst.

She stood, making sure she wasn't in front of a window. Now would have been a great time to have a phone to call 911. But she didn't have it. She stole to the back of the house, ducking under the windows, looking for her car. She knew it wasn't on the street in front, since Jackson hadn't seen it there. If he had, he would have known she was inside.

As she came to the corner of the house, ready to enter the backyard, she heard voices—and stopped. They were the voices of Arlen and Walter, she was sure. She had heard Walter often enough recently and Arlen's rasp was distinctive. She didn't dare peek around the corner. They might see her. She stood perfectly still and listened. They hadn't heard her yet.

"No, I'm not your friend," Arlen said, chuckling. The sound of it gave Tally chills. It wasn't a friendly, happy sound.

"Come on, Arlen, there's enough for both of us." That was Walter. He sounded hoarse.

"You weren't going to share, though, were you? You were going to take them all for yourself, just like that Sutton fellow."

They must be fighting over the jade, Tally thought.

"No, no! I just wanted to get them. I didn't know they were there until after the window was broken."

"I don't believe you." Arlen's rasp was quiet, and cold. It gave Tally a hollow, empty feeling behind her breastbone.

Tally heard a smack and a low "Oof!" Arlen had hit Walter somewhere that hurt. She was confused. Those two weren't in cahoots?

"That jade belongs to Thet's family and goes to my shop," Arlen growled. "None of it belongs to you. I know some is still missing. Where is it? I had the basket shop checked tonight and it's not there."

Tally heard another blow connecting with a body and another grunt of pain.

"But you have all of it now." Walter was almost sobbing. Or maybe he *was* sobbing. "There is no more. I put it in the basement. All of it. And we hauled it up. You and Thet counted it."

Another blow and another sound of pain.

"No, it's not all there. Thet and Win say some of it is missing. If you're not going to tell me, I'll have to find it for myself. We know exactly how much there was. You must think we're stupid. We're not."

"You should be careful, Arlen," Walter was choking. "Thet killed Sutton."

"I killed Sawyer Sutton. It was easy, since he's my second cousin. He never thought a thing of showing me what he had. And I'm not afraid to get rid of you. Goodbye, Walter Wright. It wasn't nice knowing you."

Tally heard sounds of scuffling. Struggling. Gurgling. Then silence. She held her breath, desperately afraid that Arlen would come around the house and find her. When she heard his boots clomping up a couple of wooden steps, then the back door open and close, then silence, she started to draw small breaths.

Dare she look now? She poked one eye around the corner. There was a shed in the small yard, not far from the back door of the house. Light from the kitchen window of the house clearly showed the form of Walter slumped against it, his head lolling at an unnatural angle.

Was he dead? She shivered at the thought. Had she just heard someone being killed? Strangled? Like Sawyer Sutton was strangled? She wanted to cry, but dared not make a noise.

She avoided looking at him too closely, crept around the back of the shed, and headed for the side street. She had to find her car. She had to drive away from here and get help, and get back before something happened to Mrs. Gerg.

There it was. On the side street, parked in back of that white van she had seen in front. She hurried to her car, but it was locked. That would have been too easy, being able to get into her car, find the keys there, and drive for help.

She would have to walk and fetch someone to get Mrs. Gerg out of that house before the remaining thieves discovered that Tally was gone.

A familiar car turned onto the street from the corner and inched past. It was a Nissan Rogue, just like Yolanda's. Was it her? She stayed out of sight behind her car. The Rogue stopped in the middle of the street.

Yolanda's familiar form got out, complete with flouncy skirt and hoop earrings, flashing in the light from a streetlamp. She walked over to Tally's car, slowly and carefully.

"Psst!" Tally poked her head out and put a shaking finger on her lips so Yolanda wouldn't make noise. After a brief hug, they got into Yolanda's car. They scrunched down as they saw three shadowy figures, one carrying a large satchel, approach the van. The tallest man got into the driver's seat. Arlen. One of the shorter ones helped the other climb into the passenger seat. The uncle and nephew. Win was older and took longer to get in. Then Thet got in back and they took off. The two women drove another block farther away from Mrs. Gerg's house before Yolanda called the police station.

They must not have checked the basement, Tally thought. If they knew Tally had escaped, they'd be looking for her. She felt in her heart that they hadn't had time to do away with Mrs. Gerg. She felt herself go limp. She was safe. And alive.

25

"Walter must have been trying to muscle in on the international smuggling operation," Detective Rogers said. "He should have stuck to small-town theft, breaking and entering here in Fredericksburg. He and Ira Mann and Kyle Meyer had a neat little operation going, breaking and entering under cover of patrolling for the crime watch group."

Tally couldn't feel deep regret for Walter's death, but she was horrified that he was so callously murdered—strangled, it turned out. She would never forget the sounds she had heard as he was being killed and was glad that, at least, she hadn't been watching.

She, the detective, Yolanda, and Mrs. Gerg sat in a green-walled conference room at the police station, putting the pieces together. It was late morning, the day after she escaped, hailed Yolanda, and summoned help to go after Thet Thura, Arlen Snead, and Min Win—and rescue Mrs. Gerg. The older woman had spent the morning at the doctor's office getting checked out and having her dressings replaced with clean ones, but, aside for the already broken bones and the bruises from the bonds—the same bruises Tally had—she was perfectly fine. Her older injuries, from her fall, were healing and wouldn't give her problems, the nurse said. She was very healthy for her age. Tally thought it was probably from all the walking she did. Tally was glad to see gleaming white splints on the poor woman's fingers, glad she hadn't picked up any infection in the coal room.

The police had apprehended all three of them leaving town, at the edge of the city limits. Two shoeboxes full of jade were in a duffel bag in the back of the white van. The men had been turned over to the federal authorities, who had been on their way to Fredericksburg to take over the international smuggling case, and a raid was planned later that day on the Dallas aquarium that Thet's family owned.

Arlen Snead had lived in Dallas for about ten years, serving as the receiver of the smuggled goods more recently, goods brought into the country with bogus orders of plastic from the Win family's fairly new factory in Myanmar. Thet Thura flew back and forth to Asia frequently to keep track of things. The aquarium did just enough legitimate business to, until now, keep the authorities away. The new plastic factory in Myanmar was also a viable company and would have given them ample profits without the smuggling. The family's greed had not been a good thing for any of them. The factory back in Asia, Detective Rogers was told, would be raided and probably shut down.

Mr. Win, as Detective Rogers called him, turned out to be a tough customer, admitting to nothing, refusing to say more than a few words to anyone after his arrest. The FBI had asked the detective to assist while they got up to speed.

Arlen Snead clammed up completely, refusing to say a word, even when his attorney showed up.

Thet Thura was the weak link. After only an hour, he admitted that Arlen Snead killed Sawyer Sutton and Walter Wright, both. He said Arlen killed Sutton to get the jade back. There wasn't a good reason for killing Walter, except that he knew too much, and that Mr. Win ordered it. Thet blamed one of his cousins for everything, beginning with putting the jade into the wrong shipment, which was what started the string of disasters. He didn't want the shipping company to know what they were carrying, so he hired Mateo and Sawyer to "hijack" the shipment and bring it to him in Dallas. He kept talking about the "extra pieces." He insisted that some of the jade was missing. He told them Mateo might have it, although he never had. The detective knew it was what Yolanda had given him, but didn't feel like letting Thet know. He did let the FBI know, though.

The shipping company manned their phones 24-7 and had been quick to come pick up the shipment and get it to its destination after the crash and the botched hijack attempt.

"That's just awful," Yolanda said. "All of that over some stones."

"Those aren't just stones." Mrs. Gerg cleared her throat. "It's the best jade in the world, most people say. Burmese Jade."

"Blood Jade," Tally added. She was impressed that Mrs. Gerg knew so much about the subject. "Have you seen any before?" she asked.

"I found a small carved Buddha a few years ago at a church basement sale. After I looked it up, I had to keep it for myself. It's in my top dresser drawer. I'm glad those awful men didn't find it." She shook her head. "To think, I thought Walter was a nice man."

"He was nicer than Thet and Arlen. And Win," Tally said. "Walter was a small-time thief, not an international one."

"At first, Walter thought Thet was a friend," Mrs. Gerg said. "When Thet first approached him, he asked Walter a lot of questions about the problem at Yolanda's basket shop, the broken window and the stolen fake candies, and he learned about the thieves that were pretending to be Crime Fritzers to explain why they were on the streets at night. I never imagined Walter was part of *that*. But Walter thought that was what Thet wanted in on. At least at first."

"Did you know those men were not from Fredericksburg? Thet and Arlen and the other one, Mr. Win?" Tally asked.

"I didn't ask Thet where they were from. He seemed nice at first, but he started acting mean after a few days. I just thought they wanted in on the things Walter stole from the houses. Thet was threatening Walter, but I didn't know what that was about, exactly. Now I can see that he knew about Walter being there when the jade was taken from Yolanda's. When he saw that Walter had been there when the window was broken, Thet and Arlen thought Walter had the missing jade. They had terrible arguments about it. Walter didn't know anything about it, but they kept badgering him."

"Why didn't you tell me you were in trouble?" Tally asked.

"Arlen said he would kill Walter if I said anything to anyone." She fished a hanky from her sleeve and wiped a tear. "Then he went and killed him anyway." She buried her face in the hankie she held in her left hand and Tally reached over to pat her on the shoulder. "No matter what Walter said, it wasn't good enough. Even after Arlen and Thet got the jade from the motel, there was some missing and Thet thought Walter had hidden it somewhere. I don't think Walter was such a bad man."

Tally would let her believe that. It wouldn't hurt anything. But to think, they had all that jade, piles of it, worth thousands and thousands. And they wanted the few little pieces Yolanda had stuck in her cupboard. Greed was a form of envy, Tally decided. As green-eyed as its fellow Deadly Sin.

"I don't know about any of you, but I didn't get much sleep last night," Jackson Rogers said. "Tally, I'm grateful you found out it was Arlen Snead who killed Sutton. We would never have matched the prints from Sutton's motel room if we hadn't caught all of them and known to match them to Snead. I'll drive all of you home, if you'd like, then I'm going home, too."

"My car's here," Yolanda said. "I'll go check on Raul at the shop. Thanks for everything, Detective." She gave him a brilliant smile and left with a flounce of her bright peasant skirt, looking as fresh as if she had gotten a good night's sleep and hadn't been wearing the same clothes for two days.

Jackson dropped Mrs. Gerg off first. Tally and Jackson went inside with her to make sure she would be all right and had everything she needed. They did a walk-through to make sure the house was in good shape. The miscreants hadn't trashed her place, anyway. Tally made sure the basement window was closed and latched.

"I'll be fine. Now, don't fuss. I've lived alone for a long time." She walked them to the door, then stopped. "Wait. I have to show you something." She went to the back of the house and returned to them carrying a small, beautiful, carved jade Buddha, about four inches high.

"It's jadeite, all right," Jackson said, reverentially, reaching out and touching it with one finger. It was so pale it looked like ice, with faint streaks of green. The jolly fat figure had a wide smile on his shiny green face and a huge belly above his crossed legs. "It would have to be worth several thousand dollars." He stroked it one last time.

Mrs. Gerg smiled, keeping hold of the statue. "I'll remember that in case I need the money."

After they left Mrs. Gerg safe and snug in her house, Jackson took Tally to her home. On the way, she finally asked the question that had been nagging her. "Do the fire chief and Thet Thura know each other?"

"I don't think so. Why would they?"

"You mentioned once that they both came from Dallas, so I wondered if they were connected in any of this."

He nodded. "I did wonder about that at one point. But Thura isn't *from* Dallas. He has a business there and visits it. He was just here trying to retrieve his contraband. The fact that Mann's son was involved in a totally different criminal enterprise muddied the water, I'll admit."

"Okay, that makes sense. The crime watchers who were breaking into the houses had nothing to do with the smuggling."

"No, they didn't. But Thura and Snead thought they might. He was confused when he learned that Wright was there when the window got smashed and the jade got taken from Yolanda's shop. Wright knew nothing about the jade, but saw a smashed window and decided to try to help himself to something. He said he was trying to catch the thief. I believe he was trying to steal from the thief and got beat up for that."

"No wonder they were confused. Walter wasn't a good person, but I'm sorry he paid for his sins with his life. He didn't deserve that. No one does." She snapped her eyes shut to block out the memories of hearing him die.

"Here we are." Jackson pulled into her driveway.

"Do you want to come in and say hi to Nigel?" she asked. That wasn't exactly what she had in mind, though.

Jackson's smile told her he was on to her. He knew what she had in mind.

Early the next morning, Tally was startled awake by pounding on her door.

"What day is it?" she muttered to Jackson.

He was turned toward her. "Friday. I have to work in a couple of hours."

"Who could that be so early?" Tally grabbed her robe and stumbled to the front of her house. She peeked through the window beside the door. Her brother, Cole, stood on the porch. She opened the door and gave him a tentative smile.

"Hey, Sis. Sorry to come here so early. I took a red-eye and landed an hour ago." A cab was pulling away and disappeared around the corner.

"You didn't drive? Where's your car?"

"It kind of got wrecked in a sandstorm. I'll have to get a new one anyway."

It was good he was done with Tuscon. She worried about how he managed his money sometimes, but he seemed to have plenty. Huge sculptures brought in a lot of money and people seemed to like his. Okay, people seemed to love them. They were becoming more and more popular and he was more and more sought after. He'd had to turn down two jobs in the last few months.

"Can I come in?" he asked.

Tally realized she was blocking the doorway. "Sure. Come on."

Nigel, probably drawn by Cole's familiar voice, trotted up to him and arched his back so Cole could reach it and pet it easily. Which he did.

Cole raised his head suddenly and stared at the hallway. Tally looked and saw that Jackson was emerging from the bedroom.

"Uh, hi," Cole said.

"Hi, Cole." Jackson was fully dressed. Tally was thankful for that. Nigel trotted up the hallway and got into his path, so Jackson bent to rub his ears. Cool as could be, the detective straightened up and edged past the two of them. "I'll see you later, Tally," he said, and went out the door. He turned on the porch. "Tally, do you want me to take you to get your car later?"

"Sure." She couldn't very well do it right now. She wasn't dressed.

Jackson sauntered down the sidewalk, got into his car, and left.

Cole stood looking, first at the departing car, then at Tally.

"So," he said.

"Yeah," she answered.

"It's about time."

The siblings stood exchanging goofy smiles for a minute before Tally put together a quick breakfast for them. Then Cole said he wanted a nap on the couch, so Tally readied herself for the day and called Jackson for a ride to pick up her car.

Bob Holt called Tally before she left the house and told her that he and Nancy were booked for a month at a large club in Sydney. Tally and Cole were both relieved to hear that.

One less thing to worry about, Tally thought. She would start worrying again in a month.

Tally opened the front door when she got to the shop and turned to go to the kitchen. Behind her the door chime jangled and she turned to see Molly rushing in.

"Am I late?" she asked, breathless.

Tally glanced at the clock. The little fat baker's hands were a teensy bit past ten o'clock. "Kind of. But you're not usually late. It's fine." She smiled at Molly to reassure her.

Outside, she saw a truck driving away. On the door it said *Howie's Garage*. From Molly's flushed, glowing face, she surmised their relationship was progressing and they had just spent the night together. She was glad for Molly. And glad for herself that she had at least one employee with a healthy relationship.

"Any news on your dad's interview?"

Molly stopped in the middle of the room and her face flushed bright red. "Yes. I'm so happy. He interviewed and they hired him! He starts in the next school term, for summer school. He doesn't even have to wait for fall, like he thought he would."

"Wonderful!" Tally hugged Molly and the young woman hugged her back.

"Mom's so happy. We all are."

Molly put her purse away and tied on her smock, her face shiny with the news of her dad's job, and probably from spending the night with Howie, too. Tally was so happy that Molly's life was going well. She deserved it.

Working on her own relationship glow, Tally floated through the day on the remnants of the night she had spent with Detective Jackson Rogers. Cole was right. It *was* about time. It felt exactly right.

In the early afternoon, Cole showed up at the shop looking rested.

"You need some sweets?" Dorella asked him, adding a flirty uplift on the last word.

He and Dorella conversed quietly in the corner for quite a while. Tally waited on other customers, sneaking glances at the two, wanting to be a fly on the shelf next to them. Cole turned on his dimples when he gave Dorella a smile just before leaving.

Tally hoped that meant the two of them were back together. This time, they should stay together.

Before closing, Lily asked to talk to Tally in her office. Tally realized that Lily had been acting distracted all day, but Tally hadn't been paying much attention to anything but the glow she felt inside.

She made it back to the office as soon as she could, hoping Lily didn't have any bad news.

"Ms. Holt, I have to tell you something."

Tally saw from the shine in her eyes that the news was, indeed, good news. She took the chair behind her desk and Lily stood next to her, shifting her weight from foot to foot.

"First of all, my cousin Amy, the one I've been living with, took a job overseas. I couldn't believe it."

"Good for her," Tally said, not quite seeing that this was good news, as it left Lily without a roommate. Tally wished she could pay her a lot more so she could better afford a place of her own.

"Yes, she's excited about it. She's leading English-speaking tours in Spain. She's studied a lot of Spanish and she'll do fine over there."

"When does she start?"

"In a couple of weeks, July. Although they say their big season is in August. She'll be able to settle in and learn the ropes and be ready for August."

Tally nodded, waiting for the shoe to drop.

Lily paused, breaking into an even bigger grin. "So I need a new place to live, right?"

Tally nodded again. And waited.

"And guess what?"

Tally chuckled. "I can't guess. You'll have to tell me."

"Well, Raul and I—you know we've been seeing each other, right? A lot."

"I knew you were dating. Didn't know how much."

"Almost every day. Ms. Holt, I love him and he loves me. We're moving in together. We found a place within walking distance from here, so we can both walk to work. We won't even need a car. Until we can save up and get one."

"I'm happy for you, Lily. This sounds good for both of you." Tally crossed her fingers behind her back for them as she said this.

"If it all works out, we want to get married in a few months."

Tally tried to cross two more fingers at that news. She envisioned having to look for a new employee in the future, but for now, Lily would need to keep working.

"You're moving in July? Will you need some days off to move in?"

"I'm not sure. Maybe. I haven't thought about that."

"Let me know if you do."

Lily swooped down and hugged Tally. "You're the best."

26

Yolanda and Tally were giggling like two young schoolgirls when Kevin and Jackson carried the drinks over to the table. It was a velvety, warm evening in September and they had taken the opportunity to drive out to one of the more scenic wineries in the Hill Country. They sat on the balcony overlooking the lush vineyard below. The vines were disappearing into the twilight as the lights that were strung above their heads came on, twinkling and casting reflections in the wine.

"What's so funny?" Jackson asked, sitting next to Tally and scooping a handful of the nut mix in the center of the round table.

"Not funny, exactly," said Tally.

"Then what?" Kevin said, following Jackson's lead and helping himself to the mixture, too.

"Didn't we just finish dinner?" Tally looked that the two men, their mouths full of the salty mixture.

"What's your point?" Jackson grinned. "So, the funny thing?"

"Things, really," Yolanda said. "My sister's wedding and Lily and Raul's."

Kevin sipped his wine, then frowned. "That's funny?"

"I said, not funny." Tally decided she might as well have some of the nuts, too. The mixture looked like it had lots of cashews and she had a weakness for those. "It's just that, they've both kept putting things off for months now. Then all of a sudden, decided to set the date."

"Dates," Yolanda said. "Well, you're right. The date."

"You don't mean…?" Kevin said, realizing what they were saying.

"Yes!" Tally said. "They've picked the same date."

"That could save you some money on gifts," Jackson said. When both women stared at him, he added, "If you can only go to one of the weddings."

"You have to buy gifts, even if you're not going," Tally explained patiently. "There are wedding rules, you know. I couldn't not buy for either one of them. The sister of my best friend and my faithful employee—the only one who never gives me any problems. She's also become a friend."

"Do you have any ideas?" Yolanda asked Tally, and they started talking about wedding gifts.

The attention of the men wandered while they two women discussed what the couples were registered for and where, and they talked about a fishing expedition they'd been planning for October. They wanted to fish the San Saba River, a little ways north of Fredericksburg. Kevin had gone there since he was a boy and he wanted to show it to Jackson.

"I usually stay in Menard," Kevin said. "We can do an all-day float and bring back a bunch of bass."

"Largemouth?"

"And white, too."

Tally listened to the men with half an ear while she and Yolanda rejected one idea after another.

"What about jade?" Yolanda asked.

"I thought you had to turn it all in."

"I did, but we could buy something jade."

"For both of them? Do you think they'd like that?" Tally wondered if anyone wanted to be reminded of everything they'd gone through in June.

"Yeah, maybe not."

The evening wore on with the four friends chatting, their tummies full of a dinner they'd had in town, their minds at ease since the criminals and miscreants had all been rounded up and the trials and sentencing were over.

Tally felt bad that Ira Mann had to serve a term, but she would probably not feel bad about it at all if he had broken into her own house. Ira's father, Armand Mann, had resigned as fire chief and moved out of town. The ranch he had bought still had a *For Sale* sign in front of the house. Dorella hadn't said a thing about Ira's arrest and sentencing. She had seen Cole a few times. Tally wasn't sure if they would get back together or not. She hoped so.

The two Asian men had been held for a few weeks here, but it was decided, eventually, to ship them back to Myanmar, where they had not only exploited the jade mines, but had murdered at least two of the factory workers who had threatened to expose their smuggling operation. Tally wondered if conditions were worse in a prison over there. She thought they might be.

Arlen Snead, however, was awaiting his trial for the two murders. Tally hoped someone was feeding the fish at Arlen's Aqua Shop.

She was seeing Mrs. Gerg often, while the older woman got over the traumas of being attracted to Walter, his murder, and her own ordeal. The woman's natural good nature was reemerging and she was beginning to walk around to yard sales and church basements again, after a hiatus of three months. Tally didn't even object when the woman brought her "finds" from her expeditions. She even bought a new shelving unit to put them on. The latest theme was animal sculptures. Tally was surprised how many Mrs. Gerg could find. The woman was resilient. Tally hoped to be a lot like her when she reached that age.

Mateo's sentence was lighter than Tally thought it would be. Raul was relieved about that, but didn't want to have much to do with his cousin.

"When are your parents due?" Yolanda asked.

Tally's mouth dropped open. "Oh no! That's right! They're coming to town the same weekend as both the weddings."

Yolanda gave a soft snort. "That ought to be a whole lot of fun."

Recipe

Clark Bars

(adapted from *Cooks.com*)

Ingredients:

     1 c. sugar
     1 c. corn syrup
     1 c. smooth peanut butter
     6 c. Rice Krispies
     12 oz. package of semisweet chocolate chips

Instructions:

Heat first two ingredients in large saucepan until just boiling, remove from heat.
Add peanut butter to the pan and mix well.
Stir in cereal (you can also use cornflakes or Special K).
Spread into 9x13 buttered baking pan.
Press into corners.
Melt chocolate chips in another pan, spread on top.
Refrigerate, then cut into squares or rectangles.

Acknowledgments

Many thanks to the people who read this for me: E. B. Davis, Kathy Waller, Jan Christensen, and Jessica Busen.

I'm also grateful to the wonderful Lyrical Press team: my editor Shannon Plackis, copy editor Richard Klin, Jennifer Chang for help with ordering, Michelle Ado for help with reviewers, and any others working behind the scenes there whom I've left off.

It's wonderful to have the support of the readers, reviewers, and bloggers who have picked this up, participated in my contests, given me blogging space, and made me feel like my work is worthwhile.

About the Author

Taken by Megan Russow

Kaye George is a national-best-selling, multiple-award-winning author of prehistory, traditional, and cozy mysteries, her latest being the Vintage Sweets series from Lyrical Press. Her short stories have appeared online, in anthologies, magazines, her own collection, and her own anthology, *Day of the Dark*. She is a member of Sisters in Crime, Smoking Guns chapter (Knoxville), Guppies chapter, Authors Guild of Tennessee, Knoxville Writers Group, and Austin Mystery Writers. She lives and works in Knoxville, TN.

Learn more at:

kayegeorge.com

facebook.com/Kaye-George-114058705318095/

Printed in the United States
by Baker & Taylor Publisher Services